I0659716

The Young Woman With An Old Soul

A STORY THAT FILLS YOUR HEART WITH
LOVE, HOPE AND GRATITUDE

By Tammy Bartaia

Sydney, NSW

DISCLAIMER

This is a work of fiction. All the names, characters, places, events and incidents in this book are the product of the author's imagination. Any resemblance to actual persons, living or dead, or actual events is purely coincidental.

"The Young Woman With An Old Soul" Tammy Bartaia - 1st ed.
ISBN 978-0-6450876-3-5

Contents

ABOUT THE AUTHOR

Tammy Bartaia is an International actress, TV presenter and author. From the age of seven her dream was to become an actress. She studied screen acting at the National Institute of Dramatic Art (Nida) in Sydney, Australia. Shortly after completing the program, she landed a lead role in a Bollywood film "The Legend of Peacock."

Tammy had a burning desire to write a novel. She always loved to write, it allowed her to use her imagination to create something special.
"Even when there is no pen and paper in my hand I always write in my mind," says Tammy.

While stuck in coronavirus lockdown, Tammy opened a blank word document and started writing her novel: "The Young Woman with an Old Soul." It's an emotional story that will fill your heart with love, hope and gratitude.

Chapter One

It was nearly noon. The young brunette woman was relaxing on the sundrenched beach. She was reading a book, resting on her raised knees. Her serenity was interrupted by a tall man with a black cat tattoo on his muscular chest. "What a beautiful day, isn't it? He exclaimed, approaching her.

The young woman shielded her eyes against the sun with her hand and gave him a polite smile. "It's a perfect day, indeed." She replied. Her hazelnut silky hair was shining on her sunburnt shoulders. She looked attractive in her red and white polka dot swimsuit.

He checked her out from head to toe. "My name is Morgan, nice to meet you," he said, without taking his eyes off her.

"I'm Georgia," she replied and wiped the sand off her arm.

"Aren't you bored being alone on the beach?" Morgan asked in a teasing voice.

"Actually, I'm not alone. My mom is enjoying the water," she gestured towards the woman, floating in the sea like a starfish.

"Ah, I see," Morgan's voice became serious, his grin faded. After a moment's hesitation, he asked: "Are you a model? You have ideal measurements."

"Oh, no," she said in a shy manner and smiled, revealing her white teeth. "I study at Sydney drama school. My passion is acting, it gives meaning to my life."

"Wow! good on you. When I was a kid I wanted to be a film director, but it wasn't just meant to be.

I'm a real estate agent. I just help my clients to purchase, rent or sell their properties. I don't have a glamorous life." He said, smiling.

"It's never too late to start following your dreams." Said Georgia.

"Oh, I'm too old to study again," he said and chuckled at the thought. "By the way, my brother is a journalist, he is well connected. He could introduce you to film directors. I guess, networking is very important to your success." He said convincingly.

She gave him a winsome smile and lowered her oval shaped dark brown eyes. Morgan asked for her contact details. Reaching into her beach bag, Georgia pulled out her business card and handed it to him. Morgan thanked her and went towards the car park, whistling softly to himself.

It was getting hotter and hotter. Georgia applied sunscreen to every inch of her body. Her mother came out of the water and shook the sand out of the towel. "We should've checked the weather forecast before going out, it's unbearably hot." She said.

"Hey, Mom, let's keep cool with ice cream. What do you say?"

"That sounds very tempting." She replied.

Georgia ran to the ice cream van and came back with two ice cream cones. "Vanilla or chocolate?" She asked her mom and licked her hands as ice cream ran down her fingers.

"Vanilla looks yummy." She replied.

Georgia picked up the chocolate ice cream with her tongue. Momentarily, she held the ice cream in her mouth. Its cold and creamy texture gave her pleasure with the very first bite.

The water was crystal clear. One could easily see the white sand beneath the surface. Escaping the heat, Georgia took a dip in the sea. From the corner of her eye, she caught a glimpse of a small fish jumping out of water. She chuckled softly. The fish tickled her toe. It was so relaxing, like a foot massage after a long run.

Georgia received a call from Morgan the very next day: "Sorry for bothering you so early in the morning. I'm having a birthday party tonight and I hope you can come."

"Happy birthday, Morgan! I will try to make it." She replied with a yawn.

"Don't try, just do it." Morgan was quite pushy.

Georgia was hesitant about attending the party where she didn't know anyone, even the host was a stranger.

"All I want for my birthday is you." Said Morgan.

They both laughed.

"Please, promise me that you will make my birthday wish come true."

"I promise." She said firmly.

Georgia put her cell phone on the bedside table and rolled onto her belly. She tried to get back to sleep, but struggled in vain. She stretched her arms above her head and rose up slowly. Georgia glanced out the window, overlooking a small cafe in front. The air was filled with the smell of coffee. The aroma of freshly brewed coffee hit her brain. She quickly got dressed and went for a stroll and a coffee.

Georgia noticed an old man with white beard sitting on the pavement outside the cafe. The man was wrapped in a grey blanket with lots of small holes. He was holding a sign saying: 'Homeless.' He had deep forehead wrinkles and tired looking eyes. The sorrow in his eyes made her heart touched. She bought a blueberry muffin and two takeaway cups of coffee and marched straight towards him. "Good morning, I got a cup of hot coffee and a muffin for you. I thought you'd like it," she said as she handed him a small paper bag.

The old man looked up at her with gratitude in his eyes. He lifted the cup of fresh coffee to his mouth with trembling hands. "May Lord send you a helper when you need it most," he said as he took a first sip of the coffee.

"Oh, thank you so much. No one has ever blessed me the way you did." She said with a self-satisfied smile.

*****

Georgia was little bit late for the party. Morgan was waiting for her at the entrance of the night club. He was surrounded by his friends. When he saw her, his face brightened to a broad smile. "You are smoking hot!" He exclaimed.

Georgia gave a smile in response. The blood rushed to her cheeks and made them rosy.

All the guests were wearing black and white attire according to the dress code. Georgia's tight sleek black gown got in the centre of attention. It fitted her tightly on her body. Her outfit was accessorised with a pair of ruby earrings. Glamorous make up and glossy hair in loose waves made her more feminine.

"You are impressive, like something from a fashion magazine, " Georgia received a compliment from a woman with big, fluffy curls.

"Oh, I really appreciate you saying that." Said Georgia. "Your hair looks amazing; I wish I had curly hair."

"Thanks, you're so sweet!" She replied. "Actually, I'm a hair dresser. I work at one of the top hair salons in the city. You should stop by sometime. I love meeting new people and making them look fantastic."

"That's awesome. I will definitely visit your salon."

"My name is Linda, by the way. I'm Morgan's best friend and his personal hair dresser," she said, taking a sip of pomegranate sangria.

The girls instantly bonded with each other. Morgan noticed them chatting together, he approached Georgia from behind and unexpectedly poked her in the waist. She got frightened and gave a scream of fear. Morgan laughed loudly. Georgia laughed with him. However, she didn't think it was funny.

"Sorry for startling you," said Morgan, still laughing. He seemed to be slightly drunk as he stumbled to his feet.

"It's okay." She replied with a puzzled look on her face.

"Georgia, I see your bubbly personality attracts everyone you meet," he said and put his arm on her shoulder.

Georgia felt a little uneasy, as if she were trapped in his arms.

"Let me introduce you to my brother, Chris." Said Morgan to her.

Brothers didn't look alike. Chris was short and fat. His big belly was hanging over his brown leather belt.

"Morgan is right. You are perfection," said Chris as he gave her a handshake.

"You are flattering me," replied Georgia and blushed a little.

"It's time to dance," said Morgan and slowly walked her out onto the dance floor.

The music was very loud, it was hard to hear each other. Morgan grabbed her roughly around her tiny waist. Georgia got annoyed, she wanted to get rid of him. She knew there was one question that could save her: "Do you know where the restroom is?" She asked.

"On the left," he answered and got his hands off her.

In the restroom Georgia bumped into Linda again. She was putting lipstick on her lips, trying to get it within her lip line. Her long fake nails were painted a delicate shade of ruby red like her lips.

"Red colour suits your skin tone." Georgia complimented her.

"Oh, thanks honey," she gave her a Hollywood smile. Linda pulled a mini perfume bottle out of her bag. She sprayed the perfume behind her ears and on the pulse point on her wrist to amplify the scent.

"The smell of jasmine is incredibly sweet; I love summer fragrances that are feminine and airy," said Georgia and deeply breathed in the beautiful fragrance.

"I know, right? The perfume is like wearing a sexy lingerie, it makes you more confident," said Linda with a cheeky smile and handed her a perfume bottle.

Georgia sprayed a jasmine perfume on her neck.

"Actually, I'm throwing a party soon, will you join me?" Linda asked.

A large grin broke on Georgia's face. "Sure, I would love that." She accepted the invitation with pleasure.

Georgia was about to leave the party without seeking out the host, but she failed in her attempt. She found herself cornered by Morgan on the stairs.

"Hey, gorgeous, would you care to take a walk with me?"

"Okay, fresh air will do me good."

They walked down the narrow street arm in arm. At the end of the unlighted street Morgan wrapped his strong arms around her possessively. He tried to kiss her on the lips, but she turned her face so he kissed her cheek.

Georgia took a step back.

"I really like you," he said and gave her a pleading look.

She forced herself to smile a little, but the smile didn't reach her eyes.

"I'm sorry if I made you feel bad. I've never felt any romantic feelings towards someone since my divorce." Said Morgan. Reaching into his pants pocket, he pulled out his wallet and removed a picture. "I have twin daughters: Sofia and Sylvia. They are six years old." He turned on the flashlight on his phone and shoved it towards the picture.

Georgia was nicely surprised. The twins looked alike. They were blond root to tip with aqua blue eyes and heart shaped lips.

"Oh, my God! They look like little angels. How do you tell your identical twin babies apart?"

"Sylvia has a tiny mole on her cheek. This mole provides a clue to tell twins apart. My girls are very funny, they never seem to get tired. They live with their mother, but on weekends they stay at my place."

"I bet you guys have great time together," said Georgia.

Morgan smiled broadly. "I totally forgot to ask you; are you single?"

"Yes. I'm single. I believe love comes naturally. I'm waiting for true love to find me."

"Sometimes love is all around us. We just need to pause for a moment and notice it," said Morgan and looked straight into her eyes.

Georgia felt awkward. "Thank you, Morgan, for a wonderful evening. I had a lot of fun."

"Thanks for beautifying my party."

"I better go home now," said Georgia and waved down a taxi.

Morgan opened a car door for her. Georgia gave him a tight smile. He watched until she disappeared.

Georgia got home a little after midnight. Wearing high heels for a long time made her legs sore, she felt pain in the muscles of her calves. Taking off shoes gave her a sense of relief. She stood in front of her bedroom mirror, too tired to remove her make up. She took her clothes off and threw herself backwards onto the bed. It was too hot for a blanket, so she covered herself with a cotton bed sheet.

***

Aroma of freshly made pancakes made her jump off the bed. Georgia followed the smell to the kitchen. She was greeted by her dog named Oscar at the door. Oscar was loving, loyal, very smart and well behaved. His broad head, well defined jaws and dark brown eyes made him look super cute. His black coat was kept in good condition.

"Who wants a treat, who is a good boy?!" Georgia exclaimed as she gave him a treat. The dog raised his paw gently and gave her a high-five. Oscar licked her face, showing his affection.

Georgia's mother, Maria was preparing tasty breakfast in the kitchen. "Morning sweetie, enjoy your favourite pancakes with maple syrup." She said to her daughter.

"I can't say no to that," Georgia grabbed a pancake straight from the pan and swallowed it down. It was so hot that she burnt her mouth.

"Let it cool before eating." Said Maria.

Georgia opened the window and let the breeze cool down hot pancakes faster. She saw the old homeless man still sitting on the pavement. She gave a deep sigh. "Mom, do we have an extra blanket?"

"Why are you asking?"

"I met a homeless man living on the street, his blanket was torn. I thought it would be nice to give him a fresh one."

"Sure, dear. You are so thoughtful," said Maria and went to her bedroom to grab the blanket from the storage ottoman bench. Maria neatly folded the blanket and put it in the plastic bag.

Georgia hurriedly grabbed the bag and ran out the door. The homeless man was eating raw beans from a can.

"Hello, I brought a fresh blanket for you," she said and handed him the plastic bag.

The old man gave her a toothless grin and tucked the cotton blanket around himself. "What is your name?" He asked.

"My name is Georgia."

The old man took a piece of chalk out of the metal box and started drawing on the pavement. "Could you please close your eyes for a moment?"

Georgia covered her eyes with her hands. After a minute or two, he completed his work. "You may open your eyes." He said.

Georgia was amazed to see a dazzling sunflower drawn on the pavement with a yellow sidewalk chalk. "It's so beautiful!" She exclaimed.

"It's for you," he replied as his grin widened.

Georgia took a photo of the sunflower and changed the wallpaper on her phone. "I will print this photo from my phone and frame it." She said.

After a few seconds, Georgia's phone started ringing. Glancing down at the screen, she saw Morgan's number.

"Hello, Georgia, I'd like to invite you to my place for dinner." His voice was abrupt.

"Sorry, Morgan, I'm not feeling well," she tried to avoid him nicely.

Morgan insisted on meeting. Georgia had no other choice than to tell him the bitter truth.: "I don't want to give you false hopes. I'm sorry, but I'm not interested to go on a date with you."

Morgan started breathing raggedly, as if he had been running. "Well, you made your choice. Just remember one thing, everyone knows everyone in the film industry."

Georgia didn't take his words close to her heart. She thought he had no intention of backing up with action. It seemed to her that it was an empty threat..

Chapter Two

The alarm clock buzzed. Georgia reached over to hit the snooze button. Sliding her feet into a pair of fluffy slippers, she marched to the window to absorb the sunlight. She Stretched out her arms to the sun and took a deep breath of the fresh air. The sun's rays fell directly on her. She had a feeling the sun bathed her in its warm, golden light. Georgia went to drama school, fired with enthusiasm for learning. She loved her school; it was a happy place for her. She had a chance to use her imagination, improvisation and do something special, something out of the ordinary.

Georgia entered the rehearsal room quietly as her fellow classmates were getting ready for the stage combat workshop. She began rehearsing a fight scene with a girl named Jessica. They had to create the illusion of physical combat without harming each other. The girls went up on stage. Jessica hit Georgia under the jaw. Georgia stepped back, tucked her chin down and attacked her opponent. She threw a self-defence punch. Her punch was so powerful that Jessica stumbled and fell down. The fight scene was quite believable. The girls demonstrated their perfect skills. The stage combat helped them to bond as they had to trust each other completely.

After the workshop, a group of students went to the cafeteria to drink some coffee. They sat tightly squeezed around the corner table. Jessica couldn't find a chair to sit on. Georgia moved aside on her chair, inviting her friend to sit next to her. Jessica gave her a friendly smile and squeezed herself in. "Hey, G, are you interested in modelling?" She asked.

Georgia shrugged.

Jessica nudged her arm. " Listen, would you like your photos to be displayed on the billboards across the country?" She gave her a wink.

"Are you kidding me?" Georgia chuckled.

"I'm serious. My best friend is a photographer; he is looking for a brunette model for the fashion editorial photo shoot. I thought you might be interested to get a modelling job." She said encouragingly to her.

"Huh! It's awesome!" She exclaimed.

"I know you are an adventurous person. You will have to jump from the yacht into the ocean for the photo shoot. Thrilling isn't it?"

"Well, I've never jumped from a height into the water, it must be scary." Georgia gave a puzzled smile.

"No worries, you will be safe." Jessica tried to assure her.

Georgia knew that she couldn't deal with the regret of missed opportunity, so she decided to tackle the fear of jumping into the water. She pushed the worrying thought away and said: "All right, I'll do it."

The girls raised their arms and hit open hands together cheerfully.

A new day has come. Georgia was excited and nervous before her first photo shoot. She was in a midst of an adventure. Her eyes were sparkling with anticipation. Georgia wanted to jump up and down, screaming: 'Yay!' But at the same time, she wanted to curl up in a ball and hide.

Entering the marina, Georgia saw a luxurious super yacht, it was like a floating palace. She removed her shoes before stepping on board. The photographer was busy with setting up the shot. He greeted Georgia warmly and introduced her to the male model named Joe. He couldn't be more than thirty years old. He was tall, very athletic and good looking. He was accompanied by a young woman. She was skinny with high prominent cheekbones. Her green eyes were framed by long artificial lashes. Georgia was curious to know if she was Joe's girlfriend.

"Hey, I'm Tara, Joe's fiancée," she said to Georgia and raised her eyebrows at her.

"Nice to meet you, Tara." She replied.

Slight smile spread across Tara's face. Georgia went down to the yacht cabin to get changed for the photo shoot. The cabin was wide with plenty of space for relaxing. Donning a black bikini, Georgia looked in the mirror at her body. She put her hand under her top and pushed her breasts up and together. Cheeky bikini bottom had a V shape cut. High cut appearance made her legs look longer. It was perfect for her body shape. She couldn't resist to take a selfie.

Joe fixed his eyes on her. "You look simply stunning." He said, becoming red in face.

Georgia was going to thank him for the compliment, but Tara interrupted her. "Joe, babe, can I have a word with you?" She grabbed his arm and pulled him aside.

Joe seemed a little uncomfortable. The photographer broke the awkwardness and asked the models to take positions and get themselves ready for the photo shoot.

Georgia and Joe stood on the deck of the yacht. The photographer looked at the scene before taking photos. "Joe, take her in your arms." He said in a solemn voice.

Joe wrapped his muscular arms around her waist and pulled her in closer. He felt her breath against his neck. Georgia cast a sidelong glance at him. The photographer caught intimate moments between them on the camera. Then he asked them to jump in the water together. Georgia was biting her nails nervously. She still couldn't get over the fear of jumping in the water.

"Don't panic, you will be fine." Joe tried to calm her down.

Georgia felt like she was losing control of her body. She trembled all over, her lips turned blue from fear.

"Jump!' Shouted the photographer.

"I can't do it." Georgia whispered in her scene partner's ear.

"Yes, you can," said Joe and kissed her on the cheek. His touch was so gentle, so warm that she got relief from a muscle spasm.

"Are you ready? Joe asked.

She nodded her head. They jumped in the water holding hands tightly. Georgia felt immensely relieved as she defeated her fear.

"Congrats, Georgia! You did a great job," said Joe and looked deep into her eyes.

"Thanks for your support, Joe," she replied, carefully avoiding his eyes.

Their harmonious conversation was disturbed by a high-pitched scream. In a split-second, Joe got attacked by his fiancée. Beating and pushing his chest, Tara yelled in a fit of jealous rage. "You are a filthy, disgusting man! You flirt with every woman you meet."

Joe turned pale. He looked utterly humiliated and frustrated, as if he were caught with his fly down. He apologised for the inconvenience and forcefully dragged Tara away. Georgia stood still for a moment, she felt sympathy for him...

She glanced at the ocean horizon. The sun was going down without hurrying, changing its colour from pale yellow to blood red. Watching the picturesque sunset gave her a sense of gratitude for the beauty of nature.

***

Georgia posted a sneak peek from the photo shoot on social media. It got lots of likes and comments. The very first comment saying: 'Luckily for me, your ring finger looks empty,' instantly caught her eye. The guy who made a comment seemed to have a good sense of humour. Viewing his profile, she discovered that he was a dentist, his name was Sam. He initiated a text conversation with her. As it turned out, Sam was going to open a dental clinic. He loved Georgia's smile and decided to make her a face of his clinic. Georgia agreed to meet him over coffee to discuss the proposal.

Georgia's favourite coffee shop was always full of energy and life. It attracted lots of customers but it wasn't just the coffee that deserved to be praised, the environment was absolutely unique. The waiters were wearing vibrant coloured uniforms to create a positive atmposphere. They were delivering coffee and cakes to the tables on roller skates. Smooth jazz helped the customers to chill out and relax.

Georgia cheerfully entered the coffee shop and made her way to a cooper coffee table. Sam was already there. When he saw Georgia, he stood up from his seat. He was holding his hands in his back pockets.

"Hi, Sam. Sorry I'm late," she said, glancing shyly at him. She could see his six pack abs through his shirt.

"I can wait for you endlessly." He replied.

Sam made her smile. "So, you are a dentist huh?"

"I call myself a smile maker. I help people to get picture perfect smiles."

Georgia chuckled. "I love that you see funny sides of things. Actually, I'm afraid of the dentist. I had my wisdom tooth removed a couple of months ago. My cheek swelled up to the size of a tennis ball. I was alarmed."

"Oh, you poor thing. If you need urgent dental care, don't hesitate to contact me. I really have gentle hands."

Georgia gave him a bright smile. She looked impressed.

The waiter in a yellow shirt and green pants brought two cups of coffee to their table. He showed off amazing skills on roller skates. Sam got really amazed. "You are the coolest," he said to the waiter.

"Thanks a lot, buddy. Enjoy your coffee," replied the waiter and slid away on roller skates.

Georgia inhaled the rich aroma of coffee beans. "I love smell of coffee." She said.

"Oh, yeah, it's the reason I get out of bed every morning," said Sam and sipped the hot coffee.

Shortly after they finished drinking coffee, an uncomfortable silence occurred. Sam wiped his mouth with a napkin and said: "Actually, it might take a few months to equip the dental clinic. I will need you for the photo shoot later." He stared at her a moment and then smiled softly. "Honestly, I asked you out because I wanted to see you badly. I really like you." He took her hand and interlocked fingers with her.

Georgia felt a fluttery sensation in her stomach, her eyes were widened with excitement Sam glanced at her with his hooded eyes. "I can sit like this forever. I'm so happy, I think I just died and went to heaven," he said, lacing his fingers through hers.

Georgia smiled, biting her lower lip. "Tell me about yourself." She said.

"Well, originally I'm from South Africa. I lost my parents in a horrific car accident. I was orphaned at the age of ten. My elder sister took on a parent role for me. My father was a farmer, my mom- an experienced dental therapist. Her dream was to have her own dental clinic. That's why I decided to open the clinic and fulfil my mother's dream." Said Sam.

"How nice of you." Georgia's heart was touched.

Then their eyes met and locked on one another... Her heart started beating very fast, her palms grew sweaty. She knew she was in trouble as she was strongly attracted to him. He kissed her hand gently. "Let's meet tomorrow again, I'd like to take you to some cool place." He said.

"Where?" She got intrigued.

"It's a surprise"

"Oh, I'm looking forward to it," she replied, lifting the hair off her forehead.

They came out of the coffee shop with their arms linked. Georgia felt someone staring at her from behind. She turned her head and saw the homeless man, who had painted a sunflower on the sidewalk for her. The old man smiled at Georgia. He gave her a thumbs-up sign, showing that he was glad to see her joyful face. Georgia waved at him, he waved back at her. Sam loved the way the old man smiled at them. He approached him and put twenty dollars into his black hat. The old man bowed his head in gratitude and said: "You are such a nice couple. Please, take care of each other."

Georgia laughed sweetly. Sam gently put his arm around her waist and slowly walked her home.

***

Georgia selected the right outfit for her second date. She looked comfortable and chic wearing blue denim jeans and a white polo shirt.

Sam picked her up in his car. The moment they saw each other, they burst into laughter. It was a twin-twin situation, they were dressed alike.

"Where are you taking me?" She asked in an eager manner.

Sam responded with a giggle to her question.

"At least give me a clue," She insisted.

"Be patient, darling."

"I don't know where we're going, but my intuition tells me it must be a fantastic place." She said.

After a few minutes, Sam stopped the car. Georgia opened the car door quickly. "Oh, it's a Luna park!" She exclaimed, grinning from ear to ear.

He glanced at her fondly. "I love your smile; it melts my heart." He said.

Her smile grew bigger.

Georgia and Sam entered a magical world. They were acting like adventurous kids: taking in the sights, eating an entire stir of fairy floss, riding the rides without a care in the world.

"Do you want to play claw machine?" He asked.

Georgia nodded her head. She approached the claw machine, hoping to score the plush toy. Despite her best efforts, she couldn't manage to win anything. "Toys are stuffed so tightly that grabbing is impossible, don't waste your time, Sam." she said and pulled a very long face.

"Chin up, I'll try my best." He replied.

Grabbing a prize took him a few tries. Finally, he won the best prize of the claw, a plush toy- Winnie the Pooh. Sam proudly handed it to Georgia. Her cheeks glowed as she hugged the soft toy.

It started raining heavily. Georgia wrapped her arms around the sweet toy to protect it from rain. Sam quickly took off his white polo shirt.

"Hey, what are you doing? Are you crazy?" She asked, her eyes widened in surprise.

Sam carefully covered Georgia with his shirt. He stood half naked in front of her. Water was pouring over his sculpted chest. "I fell in love with you at first sight," he said, looking into her eyes. He grabbed her right hand and placed her open palm on his chest.

Georgia hugged him so tightly, she felt almost out of breath. She gave him a silent assurance. Romantic chemistry led to the first kiss. Georgia stretched to her tiptoes as he was very tall. He gently held the sides of her neck and brought her head up to his. She slightly opened her lips to welcome his.

The rain got heavier. The happy couple ran to the car. He opened the back-sit door for her. Georgia's clothes were soaking wet.

"You're drenched," said Sam. He leaned forward and took off her wet shoes.

Georgia smiled shyly. Sam licked the wet rain drops off her neck. His hands ran slowly up into her hair. "Do you love me too?" He asked, smiling.

She nodded …

"Don't nod your head, just say it."

"I love you, Sam" she whispered in his ear.

"Let's have a little music," he said, turning the CD player volume up.

Sam gently took off her shirt, underneath she had on a white lace bra. He unhooked her bra and pressed his wet body against hers.

He sucked her neck strongly, giving her a love bite. She shivered as he touched her. She saw him unbuckling the belt on his trousers and got freaked out. "Sam, I've never had sex before, I'm a virgin." She whispered in his ear.

Sam smiled warmly as he met her gaze. "Shhh! Relax, I won't do anything to hurt you. I will make you feel special," he said and ran his lips on her skin towards her ear.

Georgia surrendered to love. His touch was warm and seductive, she felt tingles, the euphoria. Her emotion was so strong that tears filled her eyes. It was like a release; she gave an ecstatic sigh of happiness...

The raindrops were hitting the windows of the car. She hand drew a heart on a misty window glass.

Georgia felt loved. She was happy she lost her virginity to someone who understood that it was a significant experience for her. When she got home, she lay soaking in a hot bubble bath. Glancing at her reflection in the bathroom mirror, she noticed that she looked somehow different. Her breasts became firmer, her nipples-more sensitive. Her upper lip was a bit swollen. A kiss mark on her neck looked like a purple badge of honour. Georgia was shining from the inside out. Even her mother realised the change in her daughter.

"You're blooming like a rose," said Maria as she looked at her curiously.

Georgia blushed. "You know, I always wanted to experience the kind of love we see in the movies. I met someone and fell in love at first sight."

"That's fantastic. When are you going to introduce him to me?" She asked.

"Sam is going out of town this weekend to purchase equipment for his dental clinic. When he comes back, I'll invite him for dinner."

"All right. I'm happy for you, dear," said Maria and smiled through her heart.

"Thank you, Mom." Georgia looked out of the window and touched the glass with the rain drops on it.

Maria caressed her hair. "It's raining really hard today. I'm happy you are home safely." She said.

They were quiet for a moment. Georgia's thoughts instantly went to the poor old man living on the street.

"I feel pity for the homeless man. He might be struggling in the rain," Georgia said with deep concern in her eyes.

"I know, dear," Maria sighed. "He is such a nice person. He smiles every time he sees me."

Maria noticed that her daughter was restless. "I have an idea. Let's bring him home and feed him hot chicken broth." She said.

Georgia felt relieved. "Let's go right now. He must be sitting under the shade in front of the coffee shop," she replied and grabbed an extra-large umbrella.

They crossed the street with quick steps. Georgia looked around worriedly as she couldn't find his belongings.

"Are you sure you saw him last sitting here?" Maria asked.

"Absolutely! See, he drew a flower on the pavement for me. It's almost ruined by the rain," she pointed to the faded sunflower.

They entered to the coffee shop in attempt to find out the whereabouts of the old man. Georgia glanced at the barista with questioning eyes.

"Unfortunately, the homeless man had a sudden heart attack. Paramedics took him to the hospital, but could not save his life," he said as he dropped his eyes.

Georgia froze in place. "I can't believe this. I saw him in the morning, he was feeling just fine." She said. Tears slid from her eyes; they were salty on the tongue.

"That's life, dear. May he rest in peace," said Maria, letting out a deep sigh.

Georgia pulled her cell phone out of her jacket pocket and showed the photo of the sunflower to her mother. "I hope he is in a better place now." She said. Rubbing her hand across her eyes, she realised she was still crying.

It kept raining. Maria put up her umbrella. "Let's go home, dear," she said and grabbed her daughter's arm.

Entering the apartment building, they saw the postman putting the letter envelopes in the mailboxes. The rain drops were still falling from his plastic rain coat. The postman gave Georgia a smile and handed her an envelope. Georgia quickly opened it: "Mom, I received a paycheque from my first modelling job. I really don't know what to do with my first salary."

"Congratulations, dear. I'm proud of you. Save the money for up-coming holidays, travel memories will last forever." Said Maria.

"Good idea. I love you, Mom."

***

It was a perfect beach weather. Hot enough to get in the water, but not so hot to get sunburnt. Georgia grabbed her tote bag and hit the beach.

The beach was crowded with holidaymakers. Their voices sounded like buzzing bees around her ears. It took her a while to find a place to lay the towel down. Georgia pulled off her sandals and sat on the towel. Glancing around, she unexpectedly saw Morgan hunting high and low for the space. He was accompanied by the adorable twin girls. They were wearing unicorn print swimsuits and pink puddle jumpers. Morgan met Georgia's gaze and walked towards her. Georgia was utterly confused; she couldn't decide whether to greet him or not.

"Hello, Georgia, hope you are well," said Morgan as he approached her.

Georgia sighed in relief; Morgan didn't seem to be angry with her anymore. "Hello, Morgan. Your twin babies look so cute." She said.

"Yeah, my little munchkins are super hilarious." He replied.

"I can tell them apart, by the way." Said Georgia, giggling.

The kid's eyes sparkled with eagerness. "Let's bet on it, shall we?" They exclaimed at the same time.

"Why not? Good idea," said Morgan. He watched his kids with an amused expression.

So, they made a bet on chocolate ice cream. Georgia took a step forward to look at the girls closely. "You must be Sylvia," she said to the girl with a mole on her cheek.

"Bravo! Georgia, you really have a good memory," Morgan praised her intelligence.

The children looked at each other in surprise.

"But, how come you know that I'm Sylvia?" The little girl asked with curious eyes.

Georgia smiled. "Your father has mentioned once that you had a cute mole on your left cheek."

Morgan chuckled to himself. "Let's grab some ice cream after swimming." He suggested.

Georgia gave an approving nod. Morgan looked around the crowd and found a spot to plant a beach umbrella in the sand. The kids rushed into the sea. Within minutes of being in the water, they got a little surprise from Georgia. "Girls come on, hurry up! Your ice creams are melting," she shouted and waved at them.

"Yay! Ice cream." Exclaimed Sylvia.

The kids quickly came out of the water. "Thank you very much." They said together.

"But you won the bet, we were supposed to buy an ice cream for you." Said Morgan.

"It's okay." Replied Georgia, smiling. She glanced towards Sylvia, her nose and cheeks were completely covered in chocolate ice cream.

The kids jumped in the water again. Georgia took off her floral embroidered kaftan and applied sunscreen to her skin. Morgan sat on the towel next to her. "Could you please put some sunscreen on my tattoo?" He asked as he pushed his broad chest forward.

Georgia glanced at his black cat tattoo. The cat's tail was curled at the top like a question mark. She applied a small amount of cream gently on it. "Your tattoo looks mysterious." She said.

"Well, it seems there is something fascinating below my surface," replied Morgan and laughed at his own words. He lay on the towel and shielded his face against the sun with a white cotton cap. Morgan had a feeling of peace and serenity. However, it didn't last long. He got roughly impaled by the beach umbrella. A gust of wind picked up his navy and white striped umbrella and blew it away. Morgan jumped to his feet and ran after the umbrella down the beach. Georgia laughed out loud. After a few attempts, he managed to catch an open umbrella in mid-air.

"Well, I didn't install the beach umbrella properly, so it blew away," he said and gave her a forced smile.

"Do you need help to put your runaway umbrella in the sand?" She asked, still laughing.

"No worries, I'll handle it myself." He replied.

Georgia joined the kids in the water. They were jumping over small waves and splashing water on each other. After a quick swim, she returned to her spot and covered herself with a large waffle towel.

"Did you enjoy swimming?" Morgan asked.

"Oh, yeah, the water is beautiful. I'm going to the changing room now."

"Wait, I need to say something," he said as he grabbed her arm. "I love your beautiful personality, Georgia. Let' just forget earlier arguments and misunderstanding."

"Absolutely, let's be friends and start from the scratch." She said.

"I know acting is your passion. If you're interested in auditioning for a feature film, I could persuade the producer to give you a chance. The film director, Mr. Thompson is my brother's close friend."

"Holly Moly!" She exclaimed. Georgia felt a glow of happiness. "Bloody yes." She shouted with excitement.

"All right then, I'm keeping my fingers crossed for you." He said.

"Thank you so much, Morgan. I appreciate your kindness," said Georgia and took a deep breath of salty ocean air.

A few days later, Morgan called her with good news. "Congrats Georgia, you're invited to audition for Mr Thompson's new film. I'm sure you will nail it. The assistant director will contact you soon." He said. Judging by his tone, he was very agitated.

"That's wonderful, I cannot thank you enough." She replied.

"No problem, let's meet tonight. Dinner on me."

"I'm so sorry, I have a terrible headache."

"All right, there is always next time."

"Take care, Morgan," she said, her voice sounded a little bit cold.

Georgia's excitement instantly turned into anxiety. Her intuition told her that Morgan would have high hopes of getting into her pants.

Chapter Three

The weekend has arrived. Georgia stayed in bed longer than usual. Maria entered her daughter's room like a joyful breeze. She was holding freshly washed white bed sheets. "Rise and shine, my sweetie-pie. Someone is waiting for you," she said energetically and put the linen on the chair bedside her bed. Then she opened the window and let the sunshine and fresh air into the bedroom.

"But I'm not expecting anyone," said Georgia, rubbing her eyes.

"Well, an unexpected guest has just arrived." replied Maria, smiling.

Georgia rushed out of bed in her pyjamas. In the living room she saw her father, Daniel standing at the window surrounded by luggage. He has got back from a business trip to Europe. He looked good in his pale blue shirt and navy suspenders.

"Dad!" Exclaimed Georgia, she jumped up on her father and kissed him. "How nice it is to have you home again."

"I missed you so much, dear," he said with tears in his eyes.

"How was your trip?" She asked.

"All good. I just suffer badly from jet lag," said Daniel, leaning toward her.

Georgia tilted her head in anticipation of a pinch. Daniel chuckled. " When you were a kid you loved me to squeeze your cheeks."

"Huh! My cheeks aren't chubby anymore," she replied with a laugh.

"To me, you will always be a child, no matter your age," said Daniel and pinched her button nose.

"Get some rest, Dad," said Georgia and helped him to carry luggage up to the spare room.

After an hour or so, Daniel entered her room. "I have something for you, dear," he said and handed her the white scroll tied in red ribbon.

"What's this?" Georgia asked as she unrolled the scroll.

"I was wondering what could be a greater gift than giving a piece of the moon to my dear daughter?! I purchased a plot of land on the moon for you, sweetheart." He said.

"Wow! You are the best Dad in the world," Georgia exclaimed in delight.

Daniel shook his head. "I'm still a long way from becoming the best Dad."

"I love you, Daddy. I'm so happy to be a lunar land owner. Thank you for putting a lot of thought into a gift. I know you are fond of planets and astronomy."

"Actually, my childhood dream was to be an astronaut. I didn't want to become an engineer."

"Then why didn't you follow your dream?"

"Unfortunately, my parents chose a career for me. I wanted to travel into space to understand the power and wonders of the universe. I had a reflector telescope at home. I used to watch the shooting stars as they had been growing brighter and bigger," said Daniel with a regret in his voice.

"Oh, Dad, I think you should have fought for your dream." Georgia said to him lovingly.

"I will be truly happy if you fulfil all your dreams," said Daniel. He was about to rise from his seat when he got startled by the loud ringtone that had a real cow mooing sound.

"Is that you ringer?" He asked with a puzzled expression.

She laughed at his reaction. "I set the funny ringtone simply because I wanted to lift my mood."

Georgia looked down at her phone. She was happy to receive a call from Linda, the curly haired woman she had met at Morgan's party. Linda invited her to the roaring 20's theme birthday party. Georgia's lips parted in a smile. She thanked her for the invitation.

Daniel gave his daughter a loving glance. "I'm happy you started your day with joy and enthusiasm." He said.

"It seems I began my day on the right foot." She chuckled.

Georgia looked into the wardrobe to find something suitable for the party: anything with beading, lavish accessories, headbands, feathers, elbow gloves. "I can't find appropriate attire." She complained.

"Don't worry, dear. You have enough time to do some shopping today." He replied.

"Sure," said Georgia and pushed the door to the wardrobe closed. "Dad, would you like to have a cup of coffee with me?"

"Not now, dear, your mother wants me to go grocery shopping with her."

"Okay, Dad. See you later."

Georgia pampered herself with a long hot bath, then she made delicious coffee in a Turkish coffee pot. She waited for about half a minute to let the grinds settle to the bottom of her cup. She put a cup on the wooden table and made herself comfortable in a padded dining chair. Georgia curled up, hugging her knees tightly to the chest. She browsed through different shopping websites on her laptop, trying to find the proper outfit for Linda's birthday party. Oscar sat under her chair, guarding her against intruders. Georgia was drinking Turkish treat sip by sip.

The dog started barking loudly, she got so startled that accidently she spilled the entire cup of coffee on her shirt. Georgia quickly rubbed the coffee stain with a damp paper towel. Hearing the front door creak open, she poked her head out of the kitchen. Her parents were standing in the hallway.

"We have a surprise for you, dear," said Daniel and handed her a box tied with blue ribbon.

Georgia untied the ribbon and opened the box quickly to satisfy her curiosity. "Oh, my God! I absolutely love it." She exclaimed as she pulled a white fringed flapper dress out of the box.

"Try it on, dear. You will shine like a star." Daniel replied.

"Thank you. You're the best." Said Georgia.

"Sweetie, did you spill coffee on your shirt? "Maria asked as she noticed the stain on her daughter's pyjama top.

"Oh, yes, I think the stain won't come out in an ordinary wash."

"Coffee won't stain if you catch it quickly," said Maria and sprinkled baking soda over the stained area.

Georgia put on her new dress. The fringed flapper dress fitted her perfectly. "Thank you, guys, you picked out the most beautiful dress."

"Wear it in good health." Maria blessed her daughter.

***

Georgia looked down at her wristwatch. She arrived just on time at a boutique hotel bar. Linda welcomed her with a smile. Georgia handed her the bouquet of brightly coloured flowers. "Happy birthday, dear," she said and gave her a kiss on the cheek.

"Thank you, honey. You look sensational. Your dress is a show-stopper," she said, walking her into the bar.

The atmosphere was really nice. Ladies were dressed elegantly. Men were wearing stylish suits, they looked sharp. The bartender handed Georgia a multicoloured drink with a straw on a vintage glass cup. Taking a sip from a straw, she sat down on a bar stool. Linda introduced her to her best friend, Romina.

"Hello, Georgia. Linda told me nice things about you." Said Romina.

"Oh, she is so sweet, we met at the party and became instant friends," Replied Georgia.

A grin spread to Linda's eyes. "Hey, girls, come on, let's dance. The music is so good." She said.

"I'll finish my drink and join you later," said Romina and pursed her lips at the straw.

Georgia put her glass on the bar table and followed Linda to the dance floor. The music moved her as if she were a puppet on strings, she let her hair down. Dancing with her eyes closed, she accidently stepped on someone's foot. "Oh, I'm so sorry," she said to an iron grey-haired man.

"I will accept your apology if you dance with me." He said. His whole face was engaged in a smile, creating little wrinkles around his eyes.

"All right." She agreed.

He spun her around the dance floor. She kept giggling.

"I'm Jim, by the way. You are a perfect dance partner." He said.

"You're not bad either." She replied.

Linda watched them with an amused expression. She was a bit tipsy; she couldn't stop giggling. "You two are so cute." She said, her smile widened, including the dimples.

The music stopped. The waiter in a white uniform brought a huge red velvet cake with one burning candle. The guests started singing a happy birthday song to Linda. She blew out a candle and made a wish. They all clapped hands together.

Georgia reached home after midnight. She fumbled with a key and after a few moments of struggle, she finally unlocked the door. Georgia's dad was sleeping with his mouth slightly open on the coach. She gently tapped his shoulder and woke him up. Daniel rubbed his eyes. "How was the party? Did your friends like your new dress?" He asked, yawning loudly.

"The party was a blast. Everyone loved my dress. Please, go to your room and get some sleep, Dad."

"I'm so proud to have a daughter like you, dear."

"But I know your dream was to have a son," Georgia said ironically and sat on the coach.

"Well, I wanted to have a son so I could play football with him." He chuckled. "The first time I saw you, I had a feeling that I hadn't been living, I had been simply existing before. When you began crawling, my heart jumped out of my chest with happiness. You are the meaning of my life, dear."

"I love you, Dad. Please, don't lose sleep worrying about me when I'm out."

Daniel stood up from the coach and said: "I have an idea, let's observe the big, bright moon through my telescope. How does that sound?"

"Brilliant idea!" She exclaimed.

Georgia and Daniel went to the balcony as it was their main observatory. They started observing the moon through the old telescope. The full moon graced the sky with dark shades of blue and grey. "How beautiful!" She exclaimed. Georgia made a wish to land a role in a feature film. She repeated her wish for five times. She never stopped looking at the moon as she concentrated well. Daniel looked into his daughter's eyes and saw how much she was enjoying the moment. He saw a dream in her eyes. "You can do anything you wish. I believe in you." He said and walked slowly to his room.

Georgia took off her shoes and carefully tiptoed to her bedroom. Neatly folded pyjamas were tucked under her pillow. The stain was completely removed from the shirt. It was as good as new. She put on her pyjamas and slid into bed.

As soon as she awoke the next morning, she made a cosy announcement to her parents. "Dear Mom and Dad, I made a spur of the moment decision. Tomorrow we are going on a mini holiday. I want to do something meaningful for you."

"Are you serious?" Daniel asked, the smile touched the corners of his mouth.

"Absolutely! It's my treat. I got my first salary and I can't think of a better way to spend my money."

"You should spend your money on yourself, dear." Replied Daniel.

"Well, I wanted to spend my entire first salary on your gifts but then I changed my mind. I think travel experience will last a lifetime."

"Thank you, sweetheart. We really appreciate your care and love." Said Maria.

"Now we need to make a travel packing checklist and get ready for the trip." Said Daniel, his voice was full of joy.

"Wait a minute, first we need to find a trustworthy pet sitter for Oscar." Maria interrupted him.

"Don't worry, my friend will take care of the dog while we are away," said Daniel and petted the dog on the top of the head.

***

The happy family took off for a mini holiday. The beach resort was just two hours' drive from Sydney. The spontaneous road trip filled Georgia with positive vibes. She stuck her hand out of the car window carelessly. A gentle wind caught her hand like a sail. She felt a powerful sound of rushing wind past her hand, it made her smile. Maria snapped at her daughter: "Hey, what are you doing? You should keep your arm inside the car at all times." She said in a concerned voice. "You may risk losing a limb."

"Come on, Mom! It's ridiculous. You always worry about things that might happen. You get scared so easily." Said Georgia.

"There is nothing funny about being alert to danger. If all of a sudden someone drives a little too close to the inside lane, you may be sideswiped by a car and in a split second you may lose your arm." Replied Maria solemnly.

Daniel chuckled. "Georgia, you'd better follow your Mum's advice. Trust me, nobody can beat her in a debate," he said and glanced at his daughter in a rear-view mirror.

Georgia laughed sweetly. "Dad, can we stop at the rest area? I'm starving."

"As you wish, dear," said Daniel and parked his car at a roadside rest stop.

Georgia found a wooden picnic table with a bench. Maria took the sandwiches and snacks out of the basket.

"I'm so hungry, my stomach is growling," said Georgia and plunged into the food on her plastic plate.

She noticed a kookaburra with dark brown wings perching on a branch of a large tree. The bird had a cute white head and a broad break. "Look, Dad, the kookaburra is peering at you through wide eyes," Said Georgia.

"Oh, cheeky kookaburras are famous for their distinctive laugh." Said Daniel. He grabbed a grilled salmon sandwich and took a huge bite out of it.

The kookaburra gave a loud chorus of laughter and came down from the perch. The bird swooped without warning to steal Daniel's sandwich right off his plate. Georgia's father had a mini battle with the kookaburra. "Hey you, flying thief, leave my sandwich alone." Daniel shouted loudly.

The kookaburra won the battle. The bird pinched the food, flew off and landed in the same tree. Georgia laughed out loud. "Oh, Daddy, I know you are heartbroken that kookaburra stole your food, but I think I've never laughed so hard," she said with a chuckle.

Maria had the urge to laugh, but she tried not to burst out in laughter as she didn't want to upset her husband.

Daniel looked very serious. "All right, the show is over. It's time to take off," he said and headed to his car.

Finally, they reached the holiday resort. The hotel was right on the beach. Georgia's room was facing the ocean. Staring at the beautiful balmy waves made her feel relaxed, it put her in touch with nature.

Georgia went to the hotel buffet. Her parents were tucking into a hearty lunch. Daniel glanced up at her from under his brows." Dear, do you have any plans for today?" He asked.

"Oh, yes. I decided to take a camel tour. I've seen the pictures of the line of camels proudly parading against a beautiful sunset. I'd love to experience a camel ride on the beach." She said.

"Great idea!" Exclaimed Maria.

"Actually, riding a camel is a perfect way to strengthen your legs and core, it will make you aware of the muscle groups of the body you didn't know you had," said Daniel as he stood up from the chair. "All right, ladies. Please, enjoy your meal, I've had more than enough already. I will be waiting for you in the lobby." Daniel wiped his mouth with his serviette and walked out of the buffet.

After a few minutes, Georgia and her mother went down to the lobby. Looking through the sliding glass door, they saw Daniel sitting on a swimming pool bench next to the blonde woman. Daniel felt his wife's gaze on him, he approached her in two quick steps and said: "Honey, I have a slight headache, you'd better go without me today."

"All right, have a rest. See you later." Said Maria.

"Enjoy the wonderful desert adventure." Replied Daniel.

Georgia and Maria headed to the beach. The camels were lying down on the sand, waiting for the passengers. They were saddled between humps. One of the resting camels was gazing up at the blue sky.

Georgia came closer to the lovely animal. She hopped on a camel and comfortably placed herself in front of the hump, hanging her legs loosely against the animal's side. The camel stood up; Georgia had a feeling as if she were taking an extreme ride in an amusement park. Camel riding through the bright sand dunes gave her a great pleasure. It allowed her to gaze at birds in the sky, she paused to appreciate the picturesque landscape. Georgia enjoyed the amazing scenery while swaying from side to side. She quickly bonded with the adorable animal. The camel seemed quite relaxed. Maria took lots of photos of her daughter riding a camel cheerfully.

They returned to the hotel in a happy mood. Daniel was sitting on the same bench, talking to the same blonde woman. They seemed as if they have known each other for a very long time.

"Do you know who is that woman?" Maria asked her daughter as she lifted up the black sunglasses.

"I don't know, Mom. She must be a guest in the hotel."

As soon as Daniel saw his wife and daughter, he quickly stood up from his seat and went to them. "My precious ladies, how are you doing?" He asked with a sly smile.

"We had an awesome experience, Dad. It's a pity you couldn't make it." Said Georgia.

"I'm sorry, I promise I will make it up to you." Daniel apologised.

"I'm happy you feel better," said Maria and pulled a hotel key card out of her bag.

Georgia kissed both of her parents lovingly and ran to her room. She called her boyfriend, Sam on the phone. He seemed happy to hear her voice.

"I miss you, babe. I wish I had a magic hat to make my wish come true." Said Sam.

"What is your wish?" She asked.

"To be with my girlfriend right now. I can't stop fantasizing about you."

Georgia laughed softly. "I wish you were kissing me tenderly."

"Babe, I'm holding you in my arms. Do you feel it?" He asked in a warm and inviting voice.

"Oh, yeah, it's a tight squeeze. I'm so tiny in your arms."

"I am kissing your neck, your skin tastes so good."

"You make me feel amazing."

"I'm taking your clothes off," his voice was low and breathy.

She let the soft moan out of appreciation.

"I'm carrying you in my arms to bed. You are so hot, I feel aroused, babe." He grunted with satisfaction.

Georgia was lost in sexual fantasy. As soon as she removed her thinly transparent bra, the cleaning lady walked into her room without knocking on the door. Georgia got startled as she was caught topless. She covered her breasts with her hands. "Sam, I can't talk to you right now. I will call you later." She said in a very low voice. Georgia quickly put on her white shirt and jumped off bed.

The cleaning lady looked embarrassed. "I'm so sorry to disturb you. I thought you were out having dinner." She said as she moved her eyebrows down.

"No problem," replied Georgia and went outside to get a fresh air.

When she returned, the room looked clean and neat. The different sized pillows were symmetrically placed on bed. Georgia grabbed the pillows and set them aside as she loved sleeping without a pillow. She slipped into bed and fell asleep instantly.

***

The sun's rays fell on Georgia's face, signalling her that it was time to wake up. She glanced at the clock on the night stand. She had only half an hour left until the breakfast buffet was open. Entering the restaurant, she saw her parents loading up their plates with hot pancakes. She got pleased to see a chef cooking waffles. She joined the waffle line. The chef put two buttermilk waffles on her plate and poured hot maple syrup over top. Georgia went to her parent's table and sat by her mother's side.

"You look fresh, dear." Said Daniel.

"I slept well. It was a great idea to come here," replied Georgia and took a bite out of the waffle. "Yum! It's delicious." She exclaimed.

Daniel cut a piece of pancake and accidently dropped the fork. He went to grab the fresh cutlery and bumped into his acquaintance, the blond woman. They looked happy to see each other.

Maria's gaze drifted from her daughter to the blond woman. Daniel became so distracted that he returned to the table without a fork. Maria gave him a little smile. "Who is that lady? You talk to each other regularly." She asked her husband.

"We just met, she is a hotel guest, honey." Replied Daniel.

Georgia swallowed the last piece of the waffle and said: "The weather looks fantastic. Let's hit the dunes. I'd love to try sandboarding."

"Oh, dear, I would love to, but I'm afraid I can't. I have a dull headache, sharp pain on both sides of my head." Said Daniel. His face looked sad.

"You need to take a pain killer and have some rest. We will tackle the magnificent sand dunes. I hope you start feeling better soon so that you can join us." said Maria. She linked arms with her daughter and walked out of the restaurant.

"Mom, we are going to have heaps of fun. Sandboarding is like a snowboarding."

"Yeah, but it's a lot warmer," said Maria and laughed.

They hit the desert and chose the sand dune with a gentle slope that wasn't too long. They put on their helmets on and climbed to the top.

"Mom, are you ready?" Georgia asked.

She nodded yes. Georgia and Maria had lots of fun sitting on the sand boards, cruising down the epic dunes. Maria indulged her wild side. "Phew! I did it. I feel amazing." She exclaimed

"It just took my breath away," said Georgia, glancing up at her mother.

"Are you ready climbing to the top again? Maria asked.

"Yes! Let's do it," she replied and adjusted the bindings.

After enjoyable experience on the dunes, they boarded a shuffle bus back to the hotel. Entering the lobby, they saw Daniel sitting on the leather sofa next to the blonde woman. He was so deeply engaged in a conversation that he couldn't notice his wife and daughter standing right in front of him. Maria turned red with anger. She sighed heavily and walked to her room with quick steps. Georgia guessed that something was off. She followed her mother to her room. Maria looked irritated, she started packing her suitcase nervously.

"I'm going home. I can't stand your father's disrespectful behaviour."

"Mom, please, don't get jealous over small things. Dad loves you so much."

"I'm not jealous at all. Since we came here, he has been lying to me and it drives me crazy."

"If you go, I will not stay here either. I will pack my bag, just give me five minutes," said Georgia.

She went to the lobby in attempt to talk to her father and fix the problem. She ran into her dad in the reception area.

"Sweetheart, how was the sandboarding tour?" Daniel asked. He looked genuinely happy. "It was fine. Are you feeling better? Is your headache gone?" She asked, there was a touch of sarcasm in her voice.

"I feel a little bit better now," replied Daniel. He looked puzzled. "What's wrong? Why the long face?" He asked.

"Dad, you ruined my holiday. Mom is very upset with you. You totally ignored her and spent too much time with someone else." Georgia said in an annoyed tone.

Daniel frowned as if wondering what she was talking about. "Dear, I haven't done anything wrong." He said and shrugged.

"Come on, Dad. You give so much attention to that blonde woman. You always find a reason to talk to her." She kept complaining.

"Oh, dear, you misunderstood me. Let me explain you everything." Said Daniel with pleading eyes.

"I don't need any explanation, Dad. I think you'd better have a chat with mom." replied Georgia and ran up the stairs.

Daniel took the elevator to the fifth floor. He opened the door to his room carefully. Maria was sitting on the bed, staring at her small suitcase. She looked very sad with the corners of her mouth drawn down. Her eyebrows were lowered and pulled together. Daniel sat down on the bed next to her. He gently put his arm on her shoulder. Maria got irritated, she leaned forward and let his arm fall down. She was waiting for him to open the conversation.

"Darling, I'm so sorry that I made you feel uncomfortable." He said apologetically.

Maria didn't reply. Daniel squatted down in front of his wife and took her soft hand in his. "Please, never doubt my love. I live only for you and our daughter." He said.

"We have been married for nearly thirty years and I've never doubted you." Said Maria.

"And what made you lose trust in me? What should I do to gain it back?" He interrupted her.

"Daniel, you act like a teenager on a holiday, flirting with a woman you just met. Our perfect marriage came down to the level of everyone else's."

"Oh, dear, I made a mistake for not introducing that lady to you. Ella is an astronaut. You know my fascination with space. I always wanted to study the Sun, Moon, Stars, all the planets. In a few years the specially trained crews will depart to Mars. Ella is going to be a crew member. She might be the first human to set foot on Mars," said Daniel with a twinkle in his eyes.

Maria's mouth dropped open. "Are you kidding me? Is she really going to Mars?"

"Yes, and the whole world will watch her journey. If I were younger, I would participate in space exploration. This could be my mission to Mars."

"I know your passion for astronomy. I guess, you got lots to talk about with her. I'm sorry that I overreacted," said Maria and gave him a hug.

"Dear, I'd like to invite her for dinner. What do you say?"

"Absolutely, good idea. I'm sure Georgia would be very happy to meet with the woman who is going to Mars."

Daniel invited Ella to a nice restaurant with a seaside view to introduce her to his family. Georgia was burning with curiosity to see her. She put on a solar system planets T-shirt to impress the guest. Daniel loved his daughter's look. "Dear, I guess, you are dressed according to the theme." He said and pinched the bridge of her nose.

Ella was late for dinner. When she entered the restaurant, Georgia almost broke her neck to get a close look at her. She stared at Ella, as if she were seeing an alien. Ella looked stunning. She had electric blonde hair with dark roots. A floral summer dress with thigh high slip flattered her toned figure. Daniel stood up and pulled out a chair for her. Ella smiled modestly. "I'm sorry guys for keeping you waiting. I had an interview with a radio talk show host," she said as she hung her white leather bag over the chair.

"Ella, I'm so glad to meet you." Said Maria.

"Thank you. I'm pleased to meet you too, Maria. Your husband told me a lot about you."

Georgia was observing Ella closely as she talked. "I'm totally impressed with your courage and determination." She said to her with delight.

Ella's face lit up. "Thanks for the compliment. I hope my journey to Mars will inspire lots of girls like you to follow their dreams."

After a few minutes, the waiter approached their table to take the order. "What would you like to eat?" he asked them with a smile.

Daniel glanced at Ella. "Do you have any dietary requirements?" He asked.

"I don't eat red meat, that's all," she said as she browsed the menu.

The waiter suggested them to try the dish of the day- the grilled salmon with pea puree.

"Please, raise your hands if you want the salmon with puree." Daniel initiated.

Everyone raised their hands cheerfully. While waiting for food, Georgia bombarded Ella with questions.

"What do astronauts eat in space?"

"Well, the space food is composed of bite sized cubes, providing a good source of calories and vitamins."

"Ella, when did you decide to be an astronaut?"

"My fascination with space started when I watched a space movie for the first time. I was eight years old, since then I've been working very hard to achieve my goal," said Ella. Her voice was smug.

"And what are you looking for on Mars?"

"Signs of life." She answered shortly.

Georgia looked at her in surprise, hanging her mouth open loosely. Ella took a sip of water and said: "I don't believe that we are the only living life in solar system. I'm going to look for signs of ancient life on Mars."

Daniel was listening to Ella attentively. He was deeply focused on her words. Maria noticed that his mind floated away into space. After dinner, Georgia asked Ella to take a photo with her and turned the camera on. Ella tucked hair behind her ear and smiled for a picture.

Georgia's mini holiday has come to an end. When she got back in town, she headed to her father's friend's house to pick up her dog.

Georgia entered the front yard as the gate has been left open. Oscar gave a high-pitched bark to express the joy. He began rolling around on his back. Georgia sat on the grass and threw a tennis ball for him. The dog leaped up to catch it.

"Thank you so much for taking such a good care of my dog," she said to her dad's friend.

"You are welcome, Georgia. Oscar behaved quite well. At first, he was a little bit depressed. He refused to eat. Little by little he got used to me. Yesterday he became super excited. I guess, the dogs can predict when their owners are due to arrive." He said. "Please, give my regards to your parents."

"Thank you very much. They would be more than happy if you visit us," she said and put her dog on a leash.

Oscar slipped his collar and ran to his host. He licked his hands and came back to Georgia. It seemed he wanted to thank him for his hospitality. Georgia praised the dog for good behaviour and gave him a treat. She walked out of the front yard. Oscar followed her, repeatedly wagging his tail.

The weather changed very quickly; the blue sky turned to grey. The gloomy clouds gathered together, threatening a heavy rain. A roar of thunder made the dog scared. He tucked his tail between his legs and started whining miserably. Georgia felt restless. The sixth sense was trying to tell her something. Her intuition kicked in, warning her to be on her guard...

Chapter Four

The fresh morning breeze blew through the open window. It made the creamy translucent curtains flutter. The cool breeze chilled Georgia's skin and awakened her from a deep sleep. She was in a happy mood for being invited to her boyfriend's farmhouse. For the special occasion she chose a sleeveless summer dress with thin shoulder straps.

Sam's face lit up with pleasure when he saw her. "How is that you always look so cool! "He exclaimed.

"Oh, thanks. I never get tired of hearing compliments, just keep them coming," Georgia chuckled softly.

"Surely you are the most beautiful girl alive," he said and kissed her hand.

"Oh, Sammy, I love that you always make me laugh," she said with a satisfied grin.

"I guess, we are made for each other," he replied and started the car.

"How far is your farmhouse?" She asked.

"It's just one hour drive. Are you nervous about meeting my sister?"

"A little bit. How old is she?"

"Kaya is forty-five years old. She is single, she sacrificed her youth for me. Now it's my turn to support her." Sam's face grew serious.

"You are such a good brother," she said, touching his shoulder gently.

Georgia looked through the car window. Breeze ruffled her freshly washed hair.

In the late afternoon, they reached their destination. It was the most beautiful farm Georgia has ever seen.

The magnificent lake with a glassy surface, large vegetable garden, orchard with blossoming apricot and peach trees made the farm look like a paradise. A tall woman with strict facial features stood on the doorstep of the simple wood house. Georgia greeted her politely. "Nice to meet you, dear Kaya. I've heard a lot about you," she said and handed her a box of chocolates.

"Thanks." Replied Kaya and gave her a hard stare, she didn't even bat an eyelid.

Sam looked a little bit awkward. "Let's de-stress in nature," he said to Georgia and whisked her away.

She felt slightly at peace.

The wind picked up and blew her dress up to her neck, revealing her white underwear. Sam was greatly amused by the little incident. Georgia gave a wry smile. She couldn't stop her dress blowing up in the wind. Sam kept laughing. "There is no one around except me, babe. Don't be embarrassed, at least you are wearing an underwear." He said, still laughing.

She just stuck her tongue out at him in response.

Sam showed her around the farm. "See, I live a creative life alongside with horses, cows, goats." He said, smiling.

"How lucky you are," said Georgia as she checked the cows and their new born cute babies.

"Cows have strong maternal bonds. A mother cow licks her calf as soon as it is born," said Sam and gave a cow some treats; slices of apples and cauliflower leaves.

Sam told her many stories about farming and gardening. Georgia looked at him with affection. Learning about his passion for nature, made her fall in love with him even more. Sam linked his hand through hers and took her to the stable. she was highly delighted.

"I'm a beginner horse rider. Which horse is most trusted, what do you reckon?" she asked.

"My favourite horse is Dan," he said and pointed to the white horse eating his hay too fast. "Go talk to him, smile. A horse responds positively to people who smile."

Dan was a lovely horse with blue eyes, very graceful. Georgia petted his neck. The horse enjoyed having his head rubbed. He nudged her gently.

"If a horse nudges you, it means he loves you." Said Sam.

Georgia hopped on the horse and galloped off. She created a special bond with Dan. She enjoyed riding a horse through beautiful bush trials.

"Well done, Georgia. You rode as if you were a part of the horse." Said Sam.

Georgia looked proud of herself. Sam helped her to get down from the horse. Wrapping his arm around her waist, he walked her to the house.

A one-eyed cat met them at the door. Georgia bent down to pet the animal. The cat snuggled against her chin and meowed at her.

"Poor thing, I've found her in my backyard. She was so frightened." Said Sam.

'How did she get along with your dogs?" Georgia asked.

"I kept her away front other pets and gave a cat her own territory. I kept their toys and food separate. Two weeks later, a cat got used to my dogs. Now they are best friends," He said. Having put his fingers in his mouth, he gave a loud whistle. Five different breeds of dogs instantly stood in a row. They were shaking their tails and sneezing rapidly. Georgia got amused. Sam gave the dogs some treats. "The speed of the wag shows how excited the dog is," he said as they entered the house.

Georgia glanced at a large wooden table. A glass vase filled with peacock blue hydrangeas was placed in the middle of the table.

She inhaled the sweet aroma of the flowers. Out of the corner of her eye, she saw Kaya watching her from the kitchen. She marched towards her with a friendly smile. "How may I help you?" She asked.

"I'm good, thanks," said Kaya, cutting lettuce with a knife.

"Well, I can set a table if you don't mind." Georgia insisted.

"All right," Kaya replied and passed her a dinner plate.

Georgia nicely set the table while chatting with Sam. Kaya and Sam sat at opposite sides of the dinner table. Georgia sat next to her boyfriend.

"Help yourself to some chicken," said Sam, putting a fried chicken leg on her plate.

Georgia scooped up mashed potato from the bowl and put it on the plate beside the chicken. Sam started his dinner with green salad.

After a moment's silence, Kaya initiated the conversation with her brother. "Sam, what was the name of the girl you brought here last time?" She asked.

Sam started coughing as a piece of food blocked his mouth. Georgia asked him to lean forward and gave him five back blows. Kaya looked concerned. "Are you okay, Sam?" She asked.

Sam cleared his throat, he felt better after drinking some water. Kaya kept grilling him. "As far as I remember, you were in love with the blonde girl." She said.

"Kaya, Let's change the subject, please." Replied Sam.

"No offence. You're young and free. You have plenty of time ahead to choose the right girl. Now you should focus on your work." She said as she sipped her wine.

Sam didn't reply. He was red as a beetroot. Georgia looked pale. She wanted her quivering chin to stop, but couldn't control her emotions. The tension in the dining room was palpable.

After dinner, she asked Sam to take her home. Sam stood up from his chair, he had his car keys ready. He was about to put on his jacket when Kaya grabbed his arm and pulled him toward her. "Sam, you're tipsy, you shouldn't drive. Call a cab for Georgia, "she said, rolling her eyes.

Sam felt awkward. "I'm so sorry, babe, would you mind if I call a cab for you?" He asked in a manner that showed a lack of courage.

"No problem." Replied Georgia.

The yellow taxi arrived shortly. Sam paid the taxi fare for Georgia and asked the driver to get her home safely. The driver was cheerful and happy. He was humming softly to himself as he drove. Georgia was feeling down. She realised that her relationship with Sam wasn't going to be as smooth as expected. She became doubtful about him. It seemed that Sam was attached to his sister, he needed her stamp of approval before he committed.

"Ma'am, you're looking sad, are you okay?" The driver's voice brought her out of unpleasant thoughts.

"Thanks. I'm fine, just a little tired."

"Would you mind if we stop at the gas station for a minute? I need to fuel up."

"No worries."

The driver stopped the cab at the gas station. Georgia hopped out of the car.

"I'm going to the convenience store to get a bottle of water. Do you want me to grab something for you?" She asked.

"No, thanks," said the driver as he opened the fuel cap.

Georgia walked past a huge billboard. To her great surprise, she saw an eye-catching photo of herself jumping in the water from the yacht. Seeing the billboard was so touching, she felt goosebumps upon her skin... She recalled her first photo shoot day. The warmth flooded her cheeks as she got excited all over again.

The driver filled up a gas tank of the vehicle with petrol and honked his horn at her. Georgia came back to the car. She totally forgot buying a water bottle.

"Ma'am, I see your mood has lifted, tension in your face is gone." Said the driver, smiling.

Georgia returned the smile back.

***

Finally, the audition day has come. Georgia was so nervous, she felt cramping in her gut. She ran to the bathroom, wondering why her body reacted that way. She couldn't calm her anxious stomach.

"Hurry up, dear, you'll be late. Your father is waiting for you in the car," said Maria to her daughter.

Georgia walked out of the bathroom, looking tired. The concealer couldn't hide the dark circles under her eyes.

Maria hugged her tightly and handed her the Virgin Marry gold necklace. " It belonged to your grandmother, now it's yours, it will bring you good luck and success." She said.

"Oh, it means a lot, Mom," she replied and kissed her. She pulled her hair to the side and put the necklace around her neck.

Georgia quickly gathered her suede jacket and small bag as she rushed to the car.

"I'm sure you will rock it. Show them what you've got, kiddo." Said Daniel.

His words lifted her spirits, sharp pain in her stomach has been relieved. She turned on the radio and began humming a tune. Her high spirits didn't last long as they got stuck in a traffic jam.

It started raining. Georgia rolled up the window. The drivers of blocked cars were continuously honking their horns. She felt frustrated. "I'm going to be late." Said Georgia and bit her nails in an apprehensive manner. Getting stuck in a traffic made her feel helpless. Daniel saw the worry in her gaze. "We might waste few hours in the traffic, so let me give you a piece of advice: take off your shoes, get out of the car and run. The faster you run less wet you will get. The film studio isn't far from here." He said.

Georgia followed her father's advice without hesitation. She ran barefoot in the heavy rain and got soaking wet.

She accidently tripped on a broken pavement and injured her left foot. She felt like someone hit her with a hammer. It was hard for her to lift the front part of the foot. She walked slowly, dragging her foot along. When she reached the film studio, she wiped off the rain leaking down her face. Georgia deeply inhaled the smell that came from moistening of the ground.

Entering the building, she rushed to the bathroom and tried to fix herself in the mirror. Rain totally ruined her hair and makeup. She used the bobby pins to fix hair bun as she wanted to hold her hair more firmly. Rain caused her mascara to run down her face. She splashed her face with water and wiped it with toilet paper. Georgia dipped the mascara wand into the tube and applied a little. She put light coloured lipstick on her cupid bow lips to add shine to her look.

Georgia was made to wait in the audition room as the other actors had gone in ahead of her. Her heart starting beating fast when her turn came. The producer was as tall as mountain. He sat opposite her in a green velvet armchair. Georgia started performing her monologue. She tried to build up her character's feelings and immerse herself in the story. Expressing true feelings, she gave a powerful performance. The producer smiled; he had a satisfied look on his face.

"Thanks for emotional authenticity. You proved to be a gifted actress. Welcome on board." He said. The producer asked her to review the contract for any questions. Georgia flushed with contentment. She looked overwhelmed and near tears when he complimented her.

She walked slowly down the marble stairs, she still felt pain in her left foot. Though she was tired, she was very happy. Georgia was holding the pile of papers against her chest tightly, as if she were trying to absorb the words into her heart.

Approaching the apartment building, she saw Sam standing on the opposite side of the street. He waved hello to Georgia and walked towards her, holding his right hand behind his back.

"Happy Valentine's day!" He shouted loudly. "Will you accept my rose?" He handed her a red rose as an expression of love.

"Of course, I accept. Happy Valentine's day, Sam." She replied.

"Romantic dinner date tonight, how does it sound, babe?" He asked.

"Sounds great. Be my Valentine." Georgia giggled.

Sam hopped into his car and sped off.

As soon as she returned home, she put her beautiful rose in a glass vase filled with cold water. "You're so delicate, I'm afraid to touch you not to break you, I love your smell too." Georgia praised the rose for its look and aroma.

Valentine's dinner date was a perfect opportunity for Sam to prove his love to her. Georgia was full of expectations and marvels.

The restaurant looked like a love nest. All decorations were marked by love. The candles and flowers created intimate atmosphere. The waiters wore red heart print aprons, they looked like walking hearts.

Georgia found a basket filled with heart shaped chocolates on her chair. "Wow! My favourite dark chocolate marshmallows." She Exclaimed. She took a small bite first and then gave it to Sam.

"Love at first bite," he said and licked melted chocolate off his lips.

"Oh, your sense of humour is contagious," said Georgia with a laugh.

Sam rose his hand to get the server's attention.

"What would you like to order?" The waiter asked them.

"Sushi platters and a bottle of red wine, please." Replied Sam, glancing at Georgia.

She gazed at him in approval. Sam held her hand. Georgia looked deep into his eyes, trying to reach his soul. She wanted to get rid of her doubts regarding Sam's intentions. She wanted to make sure they were on the same page. Sam sensed her tension. "Babe, are you okay? You look a little bit off." He said.

"I wish I could tiptoe into your soul and see what's going on inside." She replied.

Sam looked at her with a puzzled expression. She leaned forward and glanced at him seeking an answer, but Sam's expression told her nothing. "Let's be honest with each other." She said.

"Absolutely, honesty is the most important aspect in relationship."

"What are your goals in life?"

"Well, as you are aware, I want to open my dental clinic. I work hard to reach my goal."

"I know that, but how do you see our relationship in the future?

Sam blushed a little. "Babe, we love each other, this is the main thing."

"Your sister didn't seem to like me."

"Oh, she has never liked my girlfriends. Please, don't take it personal. Elder sisters are always protective," said Sam, wiping sweat from his forehead with a napkin.

They were in a middle of conversation when the waiter brought sushi platters. Sushi was heart- shaped specially for the Valentine's day. Georgia didn't touch her food as she was very tense. "Sam, are you ready for a serious relationship? Are you ready to be with me when things get difficult?" She asked in an anxious tone. Her mouth was dry and she licked her lips.

Sam paused. Georgia wanted him to say that he was deeply in love with her and was ready to take things to the next level. Instead of that, Sam responded in a rough manner: "This is the exact question which I expected you to ask. He took a sip of red wine and after a moment's hesitation said: "I think it's too early to talk about serious relationship. To be honest, I can't take any responsibility right now. Let's not complicate things."

Georgia got heartbroken. Sam noticed a sad look on her face. He took her hand and kissed it gently. "Babe, I need time, maybe years to jump into a serious relationship. A girl should deserve me."

Georgia got perplexed. She pulled her hand free and stood up from the chair. "I think it's time for us to say goodbye to each other and move on," she said in a near to tears voice and rushed out of the restaurant.

Sam quickly paid the bill and ran after her. "Babe, I didn't mean to hurt you. Can't you take a joke? I love you."

Georgia quickened her step. She saw a cab approaching her. The roof top sign was illuminated, she knew the cab was vacant. She hopped into the car and gave directions to the driver.

Chapter Five

Georgia stood by the balcony door looking at the elegantly dressed ladies wearing haute couture hats. It seemed they were going to attend the horse racing event. The ladies were confidently walking down the street. Georgia leaned forward on the balcony so she could see them better. She was invited to the horse racing event by her friends, though she wasn't as excited as those well-dressed women.

After break up with her boyfriend, she got struck with sadness. Georgia recalled all sweet memories from the past associated with Sam: those late night calls, romance in texts, those hugs and kisses. She glanced at the plush toy- Winnie the pooh, sitting on the top of her wardrobe. It was the first gift from Sam. She got so angry with herself that she only remembered good times after a breakup. She desperately needed to get over him. Georgia climbed up on a chair to reach the plush toy. She placed the toy in the wardrobe and shut the door tightly, not allowing air to pass through. She had a feeling she closed the door of her heart to him.

Georgia started getting ready for the horse racing event. She didn't put much effort into her appearance. Her white vintage shoes perfectly matched with her lemon yellow short sleeved dress. She preferred wearing her hair loose and didn't bother to wear any make up.

Georgia walked along in the joyful carnival atmosphere with wide curious eyes. Gorgeous women looked fabulous in their outfits. They wore beautiful dresses accessorised with pearls, fancy gloves and vintage handbags. Most race bettors were women. Linda greeted her with open arms. "So glad to see you here."

"Likewise, you look pretty." Replied Georgia.

"Why aren't you wearing a hat?" Linda arched her eyebrows as she asked.

Georgia felt awkward.

"Wearing a hat on a race day is a very important tradition. We have to honour a tradition that dates back years ago," said Linda, looking at herself in the small mirror. She secured her pink floral hat to her head with a hatpin.

"I'll keep it in mind for the next time." Said Georgia.

"It's okay, honey. Please, join us in our circle of friends." She elbowed her way to the crowd.

Romina met Georgia with a big hug. She was wearing a yellow hat and dark blue dress that matched to her eye colour.

"Georgia, you look down. Is everything, all right?" Romina asked as she lowered her glasses.

"Well, I broke up with my boyfriend but now I'm fine." Replied Georgia.

"I'm sorry to hear that, dear. Don't give up on love just because someone broke your heart. You need to forget him and move on. As they say: your ex should never be your next." Romina motivated her.

Georgia didn't say anything, she just smiled slightly. Her mood lifted a little.

The flag dropped and the horses took off. Ladies watched the race together from the distance. Linda pulled the ivory binoculars out of her handbag and handed it to Georgia. "This is the best binoculars for horse racing," She said.

Georgia looked through it. "I chose a light brown horse to cheer for." She said confidently.

"That's great. By the way, do you know who is the owner of that horse?" Linda asked.

"I have no idea." Georgia shrugged her shoulders.

"The horse named Caramel belongs to Jim, the grey-haired man you met at my birthday party."

"Oh, really? Caramel is a such a nice horse; I hope he wins." Said Georgia and cheered for him loudly: "Go Caramel, Go! You are my top pick."

Romina chose her favourite white horse. "Go Snow white, Go! Don't let me down." She shouted at the top of her lungs.

The horses have gone over the first jump. Snow white was in the lead with another reddish one, very close to the finish line. Caramel came last in the race.

After the race has finished, Jim approached Georgia with a smile. He was neatly and stylishly dressed. His dark blue suit looked expensive and the white silk tie added a touch of elegance. "Hello, Georgia." He greeted her.

"Hi, Jim. It's a pity Caramel lost a race." She said.

"No worries, just seeing your face made my day happy." Replied Jim. He took her tiny hand and kissed it.

Linda chuckled. "Jim, you are so smitten by Georgia you even don't care if your horse lost the race," she said and touched her right earlobe. "Oh, damn it! I've lost my favourite diamond earing." She said with a worried look on her face.

"Please, don't be sad, we will find it together." Said Jim.

"I think I accidently dropped it somewhere, but I didn't hear it bounce on the floor." Said Linda.

"We need to split up and search different areas," suggested Georgia.

Jim put on his glasses to find the tiny earing. Georgia was looking for the earing very slowly and cautiously. After fifteen minutes of searching, she noticed a sparkling diamond in the grass. It was shining brightly in the sunlight. "I found it!" Georgia exclaimed.

"Oh, my God! Georgia, you are amazing! You made my day. This pair of earrings are the last gift my father gave me. He died from leukemia in Greece last year. I even couldn't say final goodbye to him," said Linda with tearful eyes.

Georgia got deeply touched. "No one is actually dead, until we have forgotten them. Never take off your earrings and you will always feel his presence in your life," she said and pulled her in for a hug.

Jim tried to cheer them up. "Ladies, are you doing anything on Monday? I would like to invite both of you to a cheese café. My friend has recently opened it. They serve delicious dishes in which cheese is used as a primary ingredient." He said.

Georgia looked hesitant. Linda loved the idea, she directed an eye towards Georgia and said: "Honey, we need to visit the cheese café. I'm sure we will have heaps of fun," she tried to assure her friend.

"All right then," Georgia said with an understanding smile.

"Jim, we accept your invitation with pleasure. "She said and smiled, uncovering her newly whitened teeth.

***

Eventually, Georgia stopped thinking about Sam. She blocked Sam's phone number and removed it from her contact list. He no longer occupied her mind and a place in her heart. Georgia decided to do internet detox, so she turned off all electronic devices to disconnect from everyday life and connect with nature. She asked Linda to accompany her on a trip to a small village not far from city. Linda agreed at once to spend the weekend in nature.

They found a cosy house, which was made in a minimalist style. The tiny house was located in the middle of the forest.

"So green and peaceful." Said Georgia as she entered the yard.

"We are lucky to have a striking view." Replied Linda.

The backyard was a small woodland of trees and dwarf sized shrubs. The dark blue and white striped hammock was hung between two trees. It was full of pillows.

"I'm dying to jump into this hammock and read a book," said Georgia.

"Enjoy yourself, honey. I'm going to set up a charcoal grill. I love cooking at the backyard barbeque." Said Linda.

"Oh, I'm sure you will impress me with your culinary skills." Replied Georgia.

Linda was in a cheerful mood. She was playing music from her phone speaker out loud. She filled a chimney starter with charcoal. "Hey, Georgia, do you like food cooked over charcoal?" She asked.

"Oh, yeah! Smoke gives meat a bitter flavour." Replied Georgia.

Linda lit charcoal easily with a few sheets of paper. Coals started glowing quickly. Once the coals were ready, she tipped them into the barbecue, humming to herself merrily. She stood by the grill, monitoring the progress of grilling chicken. She waited until chicken skin was crispy.

"Yum! I love smoke scent from the barbecue," said Georgia as she approached her friend.

Linda turned the chicken pieces over and basted them with barbecue sauce. She grilled potatoes and corn alongside the chicken. The girls sat at the round outdoor dining table, enjoying each other's company.

"It was terrific idea to come here." Said Linda.

"We need to visit this place more often," said Georgia as she took a bite of grilled chicken. "Oh, it's simply delicious, you are good at everything."

Linda smiled with pleasure at being praised.

The girls spent the whole night chatting. They watched the sunrise together, a magnificent display of red and orange colours in the sky. Watching the beautiful sunrise helped Georgia find the light within herself. She wanted to stop the time and capture the wonderful moment. Georgia had a peaceful smile on her face. She felt the chill of dawn on her skin. The fresh air rejuvenated her mind and made her feel energised and refreshed. Georgia and her friend took a quick nap on the first floor sleeping porch.

The second Georgia opened her eyes, she said: "Let's go hiking."

Linda nodded approvingly. She put two bottles of water and a navigation map in her hiking bag. After quick breakfast, they headed to the forest.

"I love the smell of trees," said Georgia and deeply inhaled fresh aroma in the air.

"I've never met a person who didn't enjoy the smell of a fir tree." Replied Linda.

The Sun was shining brightly. It warmed Georgia's heart and soul. It seemed the beautiful green forest welcomed her. She ran through the trees like a child. "Linda, can you hear birds singing?" Georgia asked, looking up at the sky.

She made no answer. Georgia turned around and found her squatting in the grass, moaning. Linda was throwing up yellow liquid. She looked sick and weak.

"Are you all right?" Georgia came closer to her and gave her a bottle of water.

Linda stopped for a moment with the bottle water halfway to her mouth and said with a trembling voice:" My period is late. I need to take a pregnancy test."

"Oh, we need to go to the pharmacy," said Georgia and took her arm to help her stand.

Linda bought a pregnancy test at the local chemist and rushed home. "Oh, my God! The test shows two lines." Shouted Linda.

"What does it mean?" Georgia asked. She stood behind the bathroom door, biting her nails.

"It means I'm pregnant," said Linda and started crying from happiness. "Will you be my child's godmother? She asked, rubbing her hands over her belly.

"Of course, dear," she said and happy tears came out of her eyes.

"My ex-husband and I have been struggling for five years. I have not been able to conceive. After divorcing him, I was desperate for a baby. At last I found a sperm donor and it worked." Said Linda.

"It's a miracle, God sent you a gift." Said Georgia, hugging her.

"I've never been as happy as I'm now. I need to take a break from work, hopefully my boss won't fire me."

"Don't worry, you won't have any problems. You're the best hair dresser in town. No one can do a better job than you."

"Stop it, you're over exaggerating." Linda was flattered by the compliment. "I can't wait to share my happiness with my friends."

"I'd love to plan and host a baby shower." Said Georgia.

"Of course, dear, I rely on you." She winked her eye at her and smiled.

The weekend was divine. Georgia enjoyed escaping from the hectic pace of modern life. Her personal battery got charged as she put a social media on pause. She got back home full of positive energy.

It was Monday evening. Georgia went to the cheese café as she didn't want to break a promise to Linda. The café was shaped like a giant yellow cheese with a bride and groom mice on the top of the roof. Georgia took wide angle shots of the unique building with her camera. Jim welcomed her with a warm smile and walked her to the table. "Thanks for coming, Georgia."

"My pleasure, where is Linda?"

"Unfortunately, she couldn't make it but I promise you won't get bored with me."

Georgia felt uncomfortable. Jim noticed her look go far off and changed the subject." What is your favourite kind of cheese?"

"A fresh goat cheese." She replied.

Jim ordered a big platter of aged, soft, firm and blue cheese. Georgia took a bite of blue cheese and said:" It has a very sharp flavour, I like it."

"My favourite is aged cheddar cheese. It's also sharp tasting." said Jim. He poured red wine into a crystal glass and handed it to her.

A few minutes later, the waitress approached them with a bottle of champagne. Jim looked surprised. "I didn't order this." He said and shrugged.

"It's a present from your neighbour," said the waitress and gestured to the man with a sombrero hat sitting at the next table.

Jim's face brightened to a broad smile. "Holla Amigo!" (Hello friend!) He exclaimed in Spanish and went to his friend's table.

"What a surprise, I've not seen you for ages, Sebastian." Said Jim and hugged his old friend tightly.

"Oh, mate, you're as strong as an ox, you almost broke my bones." Replied Sebastian and laughed out loud.

Jim invited him to sit at his table. Sebastian was wearing full beard and whiskers. He was holding an eagle head ivory walking cane in his right hand.

"Georgia, let me introduce you to my friend, Sebastian. He is a very talented Spanish artist." Said Jim.

"Como estas, senior?" (How are you, sir?) She asked Sebastian in Spanish.

The artist got impressed with Georgia." Do you speak Spanish, dear?" He asked.

"Yes, I do. My hobby is learning languages." She said and smiled in a shy manner.

Georgia and Sebastian started talking to each other in Spanish. They were so deep into the conversation that they became unaware of their surroundings. Jim couldn't understand a word. He felt like an outsider. He tinkled a glass to gain their attention. "Let's toast to our reunion!" He exclaimed, raising a glass.

"Cheers!" They said together and clinked glasses.

"Tell me about your life, mate." Sebastian asked his friend.

"Well, it's been four years after my wife died. I suffered a lot, wasn't sure if pain would ever end. Now stage of depression is gone, I overcame the grief from my wife's death. It's time to move on," he said with a sigh.

"Oh, I'm so sorry to hear about your loss. How is your daughter? She must be a big girl now." Replied Sebastian.

"My daughter is studying law in the UK. We only get to see each other during the holidays. I own my horse business. I get enjoyment from the time I spend with my beautiful horses." Said Jim.

"That's fantastic! By the way, I have an exhibition coming up soon. You and Georgia should definitely attend."

Georgia's eyes brightened with interest. "Thank you so much, sir. I would appreciate that." She said.

Sebastian gave her a curious look." Your eyes are so deep and powerful. I can sense a positive energy field around you. Can I make a portrait of yourself? He asked and looked her in the eyes.

"It would be an honour for me, sir." Said Georgia.

"Great! We should meet up soon. Now if you excuse me, I will leave as I have to wake up early tomorrow." Said Sebastian. He shook hands with both of them and left.

Georgia glanced at her wristwatch. "Oh, it's too late, I'm afraid I have to go home. Thank you for a lovely evening, Jim," she said and grabbed her purse.

"Thank you, Georgia. You made me smile today, I have almost forgotten how to smile." He replied.

Chapter Six

Meanwhile, Summer gave way to autumn. There was a chill in the air. The leaves started falling off trees. Georgia stood in the street watching children jump in the leaf piles. They were picking up the autumn leaves that had blown to the ground. The kids were throwing them at passing cars. Georgia enjoyed the first day of autumn. She walked on the gold-coloured leaves carpet lightly, she could hear the dry leaves crackling under her feet. When she reached Sebastian's art studio, she was thrilled to bits. Sebastian gave her a warm and firm handshake. "Welcome to my world, please make yourself at home."

The studio was a reflection of the artist's soul, mystical and symbolic. The high ceiling room with panoramic windows helped the artist to see the true nature of his colours. An antique wooden writing desk stood beside the marble fireplace. The desk was a mess, it was overflowed with drawing sketches, wrinkled papers and lots of unopened envelopes. The dark brown old-fashioned bookcase was placed against the wall. It was filled with books and angel statues. There were three paintings on the wall: a magnificent peacock painting, fluffy white dandelion and huge white wings.

Sebastian came closer to Georgia to study her face. "Please, go to the bathroom and wash your face properly. I don't need your makeup at all," he said with a serious expression on his face.

Georgia got embarrassed. She put a lot of effort into her appearance as she wanted to look pretty.

"It's not a photo shoot, dear. I'm not looking for a visual representation of a person. A good portrait should tell a story of a person's life.

I chose you because I see you, I see your soul. Do you know what I mean?" He asked.

"Yes, sir," she nodded in understanding. Georgia obediently went to the bathroom to remove her makeup.

A few minutes later, she came back. Overwashing and overscrabbing her face gave her skin dry, reddish patches. Georgia couldn't find a chair in the studio. She looked around awkwardly.

"Please, sit down on the floor," said Sebastian and gestured towards the carpet with his chin.

She sat cross- legged on the dark red Persian carpet. Sebastian gave her a glance of humble inquiry. "Are you comfortable?" He asked.

"Oh, yes," she nodded her head slowly.

"Now relax and start searching your soul, dig deep into it. Examine your thoughts and feelings. Your eyes will open the door to your soul, spread your soul wings and fly. I will try to convey your emotions into my artwork." He said.

Georgia took a deep breath. She looked at the dandelion painting. It took her mind back to her childhood memories: Little Georgia had been running barefoot through a field of dandelions. She blew on dandelion fluff with her eyes closed and made a wish to became an actress. She had blown all the seeds off a dandelion with a single breath.

Sebastian's voice brought her back to reality." You're doing a great job." He encouraged her.

Georgia's facial expression was peaceful.

"I'm going to do something no one has ever done before." Said Sebastian.

"I can't wait to see your work." She replied.

"I'm perfectionist. I'm not afraid to ruin my good painting for the chance at a better one. I'm sure Your portrait will be unique. I found my muse-it's you." He said and chuckled.

Georgia blushed in delight. Sebastian dried his sweaty forehead with a handkerchief and said: "Let's call it a day. I have some errands to run. I will see you tomorrow, Same time, same place."

"Sure, I'm eagerly looking forward to it." Replied Georgia. "Hasta la vista." (See you later,") she said in Spanish. Grabbing her bag, she flew down the stairs.

The next day, Georgia went to the art studio at the agreed time. Sebastian stood in the hallway. "You seem to be a very punctual person." He said.

Georgia smiled, crinkling her tiny nose. She uncapped the thermos and was about to fill the mug with fresh coffee when Sebastian held up his index finger. "No food or drink in my studio." He said and pointed at the sign posted on the door.

Georgia timidly glanced towards the door. She saw a prohibition sign, cup and cutlery in red circle with a red bar across it. "Oh, I'm so sorry, I didn't notice it," she said and put the thermos in her bag.

"All right, dear. Let's continue where we left off," he said and picked up his brush.

Georgia sat down on the carpet in front of him. Sebastian started painting with the brush he liked most. His fingers were thin with big knuckles. The artist worked with his mouth slightly open, he squinted his eyes for a better look.

After several hours of hard work, he asked her if she was feeling tired. She shook her head side to side as a way of saying no. Georgia gazed at the stack of unopened envelopes on the table. She couldn't help herself asking him a question: " Sir, if I may ask, why don't you open those envelopes?"

Sebastian didn't say anything, just scowled at her with suffering in his eyes. Georgia felt awkward. "I'm sorry if I'm annoying." She said.

"Hm, you want me to tell you the story I've never told anyone?" He smiled, lifting his eyebrows at her.

"Yes, I can hold a secret until death!" She exclaimed.

Sebastian set his brushes aside. Looking through the window, he went to his memories: "During the second world war children had to grow up quickly. I had to look after myself and my little brother while my mother worked. We had to live in fear from the constant threat of air raids. I lived in Spain, Barcelona. My grandfather was a Spanish diplomat. He was the kindest and generous person I've ever met in my life. He helped the poor Hungarian Jewish family by providing them Spanish passports and saving them from deportation to the Auschwitz concentration camp. The Jewish people had a very long and unique experience in Spain. My grandfather gave a shelter to the Jewish family. They were nice people. The couple had a very beautiful daughter, Rebecca. I was fifteen years old and fell in love with her at first sight."

"How did she look like?" Georgia interrupted him.

"Rebecca had a long red braid. Her face was white as snow with freckles. I was captivated by her freshness and beauty. She was also completely in love with me. We used to meet secretly in the basement.

I painted her seated nude on the sofa. Her red hair was long and thick enough to cover her breasts. I gave her the painting as a gift."

"What happened next?" Georgia asked with widened eyes.

"My grandpa discovered my passion for painting. He sent me to Italy to study at art school. I was attending drawing classes at school, but my heart and soul was with Rebecca. We wrote letters to each other frequently. I kept writing about the things that was hard to say out loud." Sebastian's eyes filled with tears. He pulled a white handkerchief with embroidered letter R out of his pocket. Georgia tapped him gently on the shoulder, showing compassion. He rubbed her head and continued his story: "I have been in correspondence with her nearly a year. One day I received a heartbreaking letter from her. Rebecca broke up with me as her parents decided to marry her to a Jewish guy they had chosen. I became so depressed that I couldn't paint any more. After finishing art school, I went back home. When my grandfather passed away, I couldn't stay any longer in Spain, so I migrated to Australia to start a new life."

"Is she still writing letters to you?" Georgia asked.

"Yes. My brother told me that Rebecca had truly regretted her decision to marry another man as she was still in love with me. After her husband's death, Rebecca sent me a letter but I didn't open it. I knew she wanted to be reunited with me. She kept writing letters, but I've never written back."

"Why didn't you open her letters?" Georgia asked.

"I was afraid that it would have melted my heart to read her letters."

"Sir, I think your heart just melted." Said Georgia. She handed him the unopened envelope and walked out of the art studio.

***

A wonderful bouquet of pink roses was waiting for Georgia on her doorstep. Inhaling sweet rose scent, she found a pink heart- shaped card among the blooms with a message on it: "I hope this gives you a smile, Jim."

Georgia right away called Jim on his phone. "I just wanted to say thank you." She said.

"Welcome, dear! Could you please do me a favour? Tonight, I'm having a house warming party. I'd like you to help me choose a cake for the special occasion."

"It will be my pleasure to help you."

"You're an angel! I will pick you up in an hour," Said Jim in a cheerful voice.

The luxuries cake shop had a vintage feel. The colourful shelves were full of jaw dropping exquisite cakes.

"These cakes are too pretty to eat." Said Georgia.

"Choosing a cake isn't easy." Replied Jim.

It took them a while to browse the selection and find an ideal cake. Jim liked a salted caramel drip cake, Georgia couldn't take her eyes off the chocolate cake. A home style cake caused her to experience nostalgia.

"It seems to me that you're fond of chocolate drip cake." Said Jim.

"Oh, yes. This cake reminds me of my childhood. My grandmother used to bake a chocolate cake for me."

Jim asked the shop assistant to pack the chocolate drip cake in a box. He gently took Georgia's elbow and led her outside. They hopped into the car. Georgia placed the cake box on her lap. Jim started the car and drove off. "Hey, there is a present for you on the back seat." Said Jim.

Georgia stretched out her right hand into the back seat and found a small jewellery box. "What's that? It's not my birthday today."

"It's a pearl necklace. Sailors say that pearls are the tears of mermaids. Please, accept my gift. It's from my heart. You're so special, deep, different than any woman I've ever met. To be honest I've feelings for you."

"Oh!" She exclaimed, she looked startled for an instant. "I broke up with my boyfriend recently, I'm not ready to start dating again. I'm focusing on my career now."

"Please, don't get me wrong. I'm not asking for anything. Just be my friend. Take as much time as you need. Don't push me away."

Georgia didn't say a word, she didn't want to spoil his mood.

They arrived at a modern luxury house. Jim gave her a tour of his new home. The house included five bedrooms, seven bathrooms, with his and hers sinks, a grand living space, huge kitchen and indoor pool. "I don't like to sweat out at the gym with other people, I have my own gym," he said and proudly guided her to his pretty well-equipped studio.

"I love simplicity of the design. You chose the perfect colour palette for your home, a mix of beige and grey." Said Georgia.

The guests were waiting for the host in the living room. They were chatting and admiring the view from the balcony. They brought lots of gifts to furnish the new home. The majority of the guests were ladies. They gave Georgia a strange look.

"This is my friend Georgia, a very talented actress." Jim introduced her to his guests.

Georgia smiled modestly. As soon as Jim left the living room, the ladies circled her around and bombarded her with questions.

"How old are you? How long have you been in a relationship with Jim?" The red headed woman with vintage cat eye glasses began to interrogate her.

Georgia supressed a smile. She was about to give an answer when the red headed woman's friend asked her another question with a high-pitched voice. "Have you met Jim's daughter?"

The ladies shot questions at her so quickly, she didn't even have time to answer. Georgia felt as if mosquitos have bitten her. They pierced her skin to consume her blood. The feeling was so real that she felt itchy. She was looking for puffy bumps on her arms. Fortunately for her, Linda entered the living room and at once broke the tension. Mosquito bites healed in seconds. "Linda! How good to see you." Georgia screamed with delight. She got cheered by her presence. Linda stretched her arms and gave her a huge hug. They went to the balcony as Georgia needed some fresh air.

"Long time no see, I missed you so much." Said Georgia.

"I know, honey. I was suffering from morning sickness."

"It must be a common symptom of early pregnancy, don't worry."

"I guess so," she said as she placed her hands protectively across her belly. "By the way, Jim is totally smitten with you," Linda grinned, a cute dimple appeared in the upper part of her left cheek

"He put me in an awkward position. Jim is a nice person. I respect him, but I'm not interested to get into a relationship with him. First of all, there is a significant age difference between us. Secondly, I'm focused on my career and I don't need any distractions right now."

"Come on, honey, sixty is the new forty. Don't you know that? No one will ever love you the way Jim loves you. He is a true gentleman. Don't shut him down. Time will show if he deserves your heart."

Their conversation was interrupted by Jim." Ladies, dinner is served. Please, join us inside."

The elegant dining table was decorated with blue orchids and white candles. Jim pulled up a chair to sit beside Georgia. He lifted a glass and made a toast. "Thank you all for coming. Your presence is very much appreciated. Special thanks to beautiful Georgia who helped me choose the delicious cake. She brightened up the evening."

Georgia thanked him for the compliment and made a house warming toast: "Let this house be filled with positive energy."

"Thank you so much, Georgia. Your presence fills my heart with positivity," replied Jim as he passed the platter of sliced roast duck to her.

"I love roasted duck stuffed with apples," She said, taking a bite out of it.

The red headed woman rolled her eyes at Georgia, expressing her cynicism. The air in the room was heavy with tension. Georgia swallowed down the huge lump in her throat and focused on the food in front of her. The desert was served after dinner. Georgia put a piece of her favourite chocolate cake on her plate. She ate the cake with enjoyment. The chocolate cake got mixed reviews: "It's so perfect and moist!" Said Linda.

"Not bad," replied the woman with a plump face, sitting next to Linda.

"I think this cake lacks flavour." The red-headed woman pushed her plate aside and said:" It lacks a heavenly chew."

Georgia took another slice of chocolate cake. "It's so light and fluffy, I can't stop eating," she said. Her voice sounded strained, she tried to cover it with a laugh. A stress rush on her chest was very noticeable as she wore a low-cut blouse. Georgia has eaten so much that her clothes felt tight and she had to unzip her pencil skirt a little.

"This is the best cake I've ever had." Said Jim. His eyes smiled up at her.

The atmosphere in the room was extremely tense. Georgia was impatient to get home. "I'm afraid I have to leave now." She said.

"Do you want me to give you a lift?" Jim asked and tried to stand, but Georgia kept him seated with a wave of her hand.

"No worries, please take care of your guests. I'll catch a cab." She said.

"All right then. Please, don't plan anything for tomorrow as we are supposed to attend the opening of the exhibition. Sebastian will be waiting for us." Said Jim.

"I won't miss that for anything." Replied Georgia and stepped out of the house.

Linda followed her. "Wait, I'm coming with you." She said.

"Feels good to take a little walk after dinner," replied Georgia and took a deep breath of clean air.

"Indeed! Exclaimed Linda. "Hey, pop into my salon tomorrow, I will glam up your look."

"That would be awesome." Replied Georgia in a thrilled tone.

***

To make herself look pretty on a special day, Georgia went to the salon.

"Hi, how can I help you?" The receptionist asked her.

"I'm sorry to arrive without an appointment, Linda is waiting for me." Said Georgia with a friendly smile.

"Please, have a seat. She won't be long," said the receptionist and offered her a cup of coffee.

Georgia picked up a hair magazine and started to flick through the pages.

A few minutes later, Linda came up to her. "Sweetie, I'm at your service now." She walked her to the hair wash area to get her hair clean and ready for the next steps.

As soon as she got her hair washed, Linda moved her to the styling chair. "What kind of hair style do you prefer?"

"Easy, curly hair style." Responded Georgia.

Linda started blow drying Georgia's hair.

"Such a cool place with calming aura," said Georgia as she began soaking up the positive atmosphere.

"Customers show up here not just for a good haircut, they also need a little relaxation."

Georgia was staring at her reflexion in the mirror.

"You will look very beautiful tonight," said Linda as she swivelled the leather styling chair around, so Georgia could see the final result.

"Thank you so much, Linda. I love my curls," replied Georgia and confidently stepped out of the chair.

"Let's catch up later and chit chat. I've been busy these days looking to buy a small apartment. Morgan is the best real estate agent; he was extremely helpful in assisting me buying a property at the right price."

"Congratulations! I'm very happy for you." Georgia blew her friend a kiss and waved goodbye.

The exhibition was held at the art gallery. Sebastian was greeting his guests, shaking hands with everyone. He stood leaning on his eagle headed cane. The artist displayed his paintings from the latest collection. The theme of the exhibition was purity of soul.

Georgia almost flew into the art gallery as she was very much excited. She looked stunning in her light blue gown. Curly hairstyle gave her a more sophisticated look.

"Georgia, I was anxiously expecting you. Let me show you something," Sebastian whispered in her ear and gently turned her face to the right.

Georgia's heart moved from her chest when she saw a big portrait of herself hanging on the wall. She became lost in the painting. It was so special that she stood there, admiring it for a long time. Sebastian perfectly conveyed her feelings into his artwork. Georgia's eyes were gazing at the blue sky with sun rays, as if she were getting protection from a higher power that watched her from above. Her eyes were deep and innocent, full of dreams and hopes. The viewers were staring at Georgia's portrait in astonishment. It captured everyone's attention.

"I feel like I have invisible wings. I'm lifted from the earth, I feel lighter," said Georgia as her eyes sparkled with joy.

"That's what I needed to hear from you." Replied Sebastian.

Jim made no comment.

"How do you like it, Jim?" Georgia asked.

"Honestly, you are more beautiful in real life than you are in that painting." Answered Jim.

Sebastian smiled through his moustache. Jim was about to say something when a middle-aged woman came up behind him and wrapped her arms around his neck. She turned his head and kissed him passionately on the lips. Her chandelier earrings were so big that Georgia couldn't see her face. Her light brown leather shoes were worn through.

"Dios Mio!" (Oh, my God!) Sebastian exclaimed in Spanish.

Jim's face went deathly pale. He seemed confused. He gently pushed her away." I'm sorry, Eleonora, I need to leave now as I have an urgent business meeting." He said apologetically to her.

Jim thanked Sebastian for inviting him and walked out of the art gallery without looking back. Eleonora glanced at Georgia ironically. "Is that your portrait?" She asked.

"Yes." Replied Georgia.

"Huh!" She exclaimed rather bitterly. " Just so you know, Jim is my boyfriend, you should stay away from him. Don't make my hackles rise," she said in a threatening tone.

Sebastian threw his head back and let out a wheezing laugh. He whisked Georgia away. "Her perfume makes me dizzy. I compare cheap perfume to cheap wine," he said, smirking at Georgia. " Please, don't give her any attention. She is just an ignorant woman. I have no idea who invited her," he shrugged his right shoulder.

"Whatever," replied Georgia with a sigh. "I'm extremely happy today and no one can ruin my happiness. I'm grateful that I had the chance to know you."

"You are my muse." He said with a big smile.

In spite of the little incident, Georgia left the art gallery in high spirits.

Chapter Seven

Morgan was throwing a party to celebrate Georgia's success in getting on the acting ladder.

It was a cool and breezy evening. A flash of lightning lit Georgia's room. She put on a mini black dress and fastened her belt bag tightly around her waist. She knew a heavy rain would come, so she took the umbrella with her.

A taxi driver dropped her off at a big red brick house with high arched windows. Georgia knocked on a door with the knuckles of her hand. The door was instantly opened by a bold man with a giant hump on his upper back. He stood there, gawking at her. His eyes were as cold as ice. "You must be Georgia." He said.

"Good evening. Nice to meet you," said Georgia as she entered the hallway. Leaning her umbrella against the wall, she saw a black cat staring at her. Its amber coloured eyes hypnotized her; Georgia felt as if she were a scared baby mouse, caught in a trap. She quickly averted her eyes to break the eye contact with the cat. "Sorry, I didn't get your name?" She asked the host.

" Everyone calls me the hunchback," he replied shortly and guided her to the dining room. "Morgan will be joining you soon. Would you like something to drink?" He asked.

"No, thank you." Replied Georgia.

The hunchback walked out of the room and closed the door behind him. Georgia sat down on the dark brown sofa with oak arms. She looked around curiously. The walls were covered with mirrors. The champagne beige carpet perfectly matched polished wood floor. Furnishings were luxurious. The cinnamon scented candles made the room smell nice. Georgia felt strange that not a single guest showed up to the party. A glance at her wristwatch confirmed that she was punctual to her time. After sitting in silence for a couple of minutes, she heard some mysterious voices coming from behind the wall. Georgia got very intrigued. She entered the corridor, leading to the room from which the strange noises were heard. She put on a brave face and slightly opened the door. Georgia saw several men in black suits standing in a circle. They were wearing domino masks, covering only the area around their eyes. She gave a quick glance around the room and noticed a bust of the man with horns and pointed ears on the marble stand. Georgia guessed that her life was in danger. She got so scared that she screamed her head off and accidently stepped on the black cat's tail. The cat started growling. Georgia stormed out of the house.

It was raining heavily. Georgia absentmindedly left her umbrella at the red brick house. "Oh, God, please, make this day be over," she murmured to herself. Her vision was blurred with tears. Georgia got drenched down to her knickers. She ran as fast as she could and tripped over her untied shoelace. When Georgia bent down to tie the shoelace, she heard laughter coming from behind. She turned her head and saw the hunchback. He was wearing an evil expression. Georgia screamed loudly: "Help! Help! But nobody was around to help. The motorcyclist almost hit her as she crossed the road against the red light. Georgia nearly wet herself from fear. She saw a cab coming towards her and froze like a kangaroo in the headlights. The driver honked his horn at her. Georgia waved down the cab. Her hands were shaking as she opened the door. She hopped into the cab and shouted to the driver: "Speed up!" She was breathing heavily through her mouth.

"Are you all right? You look like you've seen a phantom!" Said the driver.

Georgia didn't reply. She pulled her cell phone out of her belt bag and dialled Morgan's number. "Why did you invite me to that damn place?" She yelled at him.

"Please, calm down. Don't make a drama out of nothing. You must have misunderstood me."

"We don't have anything in common anymore." She said and ended the conversation.

Georgia was still in tears when she reached home. She slowly slid into her room as she didn't want her parents to see her devastated face. Her cell phone rang, interrupting her thoughts. She answered the phone without looking at the screen, "What do you want from me, Morgan?" She yelled.

"It's Jim, darling. Sorry to disturb you this late, I need to talk to you."

Georgia paused for a moment to catch her breath and said:" Okay, let's meet tomorrow at the coffee shop near my place."

Georgia threw herself down on her bed, curling up into a ball and sobbed. She couldn't get rid of the fear that slid through her. She went to sleep with lights on as she was still very scared.

The bedside lamp was on all night. The light bulb couldn't handle the heat, it spontaneously exploded and frightened her. When she realised that the power surge caused the light bulb to break, she got relieved. Georgia carefully picked up the shards of glass and placed them in a double-layered plastic bag. Skipping her breakfast, she hurried off to see Jim.

As she entered the coffee shop, memories of her ex-boyfriend, Sam came flooding back. This was the place where they met for the first time. Georgia was extremely happy back then; radiating liveliness...

"Georgia! I'm right here." Jim's voice brought her out of her thoughts. Jim was sitting at a cooper table. He quickly pulled out a chair for her. Georgia sensed his discomfort; Jim was nervous around her.

"Thanks for coming, Georgia. I'd like to apologise for the incident that happened at the art gallery. Elenora is my ex- girlfriend. I don't have any feelings for her anymore. She was drunk, that's why she behaved inappropriately. She won't disturb you again, I promise."

"No worries, Jim. Just forget it."

"I think I am in love with you, Georgia."

"But we have already talked about this," she looked a little annoyed. She wanted to say something, but Jim didn't want to hear it, he put his hand over her mouth to stop her.

"Dear, one thing I am certain of is that I want to be with you." He said.

"I'm sorry, but unfortunately I can't be with you. I'm focused on my acting career now. Besides, I don't feel comfortable in your circle of friends. I respect you a lot and I don't want to waste your time." Said Georgia.

Jim tensed up. "Oh, dear, don't say that. My friends aren't mean people. Please, don't judge them on first impressions. You are very important to me and I don't want to lose you."

Georgia interrupted him: "Honestly, I don't have any feelings for you, I'm very sorry."

Jim didn't give up on her easily: "You possess all the qualities I want in a woman," he said, squeezing her hand tightly.

Georgia rose up from the chair. Jim also stood up from his seat quickly. He caught her under his arms and pulled her against his chest. He held her so tight that she was unable to move. Jim felt her heartbeat. He couldn't resist temptation and pressed his lips against hers. Georgia turned her head away from him and unexpectedly caught a glimpse of Morgan staring at her. He was standing at the counter, waiting for the coffee to be made. Georgia felt her whole body sag. She pushed Jim back and freed herself from the arm wrapped around her.

A barista handed Morgan a take away coffee cup. Morgan gave a threatening stare at Georgia and left the coffee shop slamming the door so hard that the glass rattled. Georgia felt uneasy, she lifted a glass of water to her mouth and sipped it slowly. Jim looked a bit embarrassed. "I'm sorry, Georgia, I couldn't control my feelings." He apologised to her.

"Please, understand my situation, Jim. I can't force myself to develop feelings for you. I hope one day you meet someone who makes you very happy." Said Georgia.

"Give me a chance." He said pleadingly.

"Sorry, Jim. I must leave now; I have an important meeting with the film director." she said and walked out of the coffee shop.

***

The moment she sat foot in the film studio, her heart started to pound.

"Hello, my name is Georgia. I need to see Mr. Thompson; we have a meeting today." she said to his secretary.

"Unfortunately, Mr. Thompson is out of town. He asked me to inform you that due to unforeseen circumstances he had to cancel the contract with you. We're deeply saddened." She replied, looking guilty.

Georgia froze in shock. Her skin began tingling, her face felt flushed. She had a heavy feeling in her stomach.

"Are you okay?" Asked the secretary and handed her a glass of water.

She didn't make a response.

Georgia couldn't remember how she got home. She fell into bed fully clothed and emotionally empty. She didn't want to accept the fact. She thought that the director had been forced to make the sudden decision. Georgia strongly suspected that Morgan had ruined her reputation. She wanted to free herself from doubts, so she called him. Morgan answered on first ring.

"Georgia, listen, forget about Mr. Thompson's film. You're an egoist. You use people and step on them to achieve your goals." He said, growing irritated.

Georgia was taken aback by his words. "What kind of man are you?! I know you are involved in a secret practise of satanic worship," she said in a choked voice.

Morgan paused for breath, then he continued threatening her: "Please, stop contacting people from my circle of friends. Remember, everyone knows everyone," he said in a raging voice.

"I can't cut off contact with people just because of your jealousy. You took the job of spreading hate," she said and disconnected conversation.

Georgia had an anxiety lump in her throat. She found it difficult to understand how someone could be so mean. She couldn't get rid of negative emotions. Georgia wanted to make her mind, heart and soul work together, so she started to play the piano to change her emotional state.

The black antique piano with candle holders was standing in the living room. She adjusted the piano stool to the right height and took a deep breath. Her fingers were caressing the piano keys with grace.

She listened to the music and thought about the notes. She felt the rhythm and the beat of the melody. She engaged both her thoughts and feelings and entered into the music with her whole soul. Georgia expressed her feelings and emotions openly. She played out her anger, instead of taking it out on someone. Finally, she found a piece of mind.

Georgia put on her activewear and got ready to jog around the park. As she stepped out of the apartment building, she saw a man standing about five feet in front of her. He had a wide face with a wrinkled forehead. His face was unshaven and grey. He gave her a penetrating stare. Georgia looked away and headed to the park. The man followed her. " Excuse me, miss, do you remember me?" He asked with a loud voice.

Georgia threw a frightened look at him. The man gave her a cordial smile. "I apologise for startling you. I'm Otto, we met at Linda's birthday party." He smiled; His gapped front teeth made him look bold.

"Oh, I'm glad to see you, I was carried away by thoughts. Do you live near here?"

"No, I just visited a friend of mine," he coughed softly into his hand. "Just by looking at your face, I see an adventures life ahead of you." He said.

"Are you a fortune teller?" She chuckled.

"Well, I'm blessed to have a gift at seeing the future. I can tell you about your past and present as well. If you like I can even read your palm."

"Sure, I'd love that," she said it without hesitation.

They reached the park and sat down on a bench. He took Georgia's right hand and started reading her palm.

"What do the lines on my palm mean?" She asked out of curiosity.

"The palm of hand has four main lines. Your life line is long, it indicates your health and vitality."

"How about my career line?" She interrupted him.

"Fate line is known as a career line. You have no breaks in this line. It means you will achieve great success and fulfil your dreams."

Georgia's eyes brightened. She really needed to hear it.

"The head line represents your mind. Your line shows you are emotional and a good communicator." Said Otto.

"How about the fourth line? Georgia asked enthusiastically.

"Heart line is about love. Yours is curved, it shows you are soft and sensitive."

"It sounds very interesting to me." Said Georgia.

Otto glanced at her with a queer; scratching his chin softly. "I will tell you the rest next time if you give me your contact number." He said and snooped through his phone.

"That would be great, "said Georgia and gave her business card to him.

Otto left. She stayed for a while to digest new information. Georgia kept looking down at her palm of the right hand. She found the vertical line running up the palm towards her middle finger, it was her fate line. She was eager to find out more about her future. Georgia was lost in her thoughts when a drop of rain fell on her forehead. She raised her head and noticed someone hiding behind the tree. She looked searchingly, took a step forward and caught a glimpse of the hunch-back. A fear ran down her spine. Georgia stared at him in horror, she saw his bloody eye whites. He glanced at her ironically. Georgia pan-icked and pushed back. She screamed for help, but there was no one insight. She ran like a wind.

By the time Georgia reached home, she was shivering with fear. Her heart was breathing rapidly. She locked the door from the inside as she was worried that he could break into her house. Georgia wanted to discover why she was chosen as a target. She put her pride aside and called Morgan, but his phone number was out of service. She de-cided to find out Morgan's secrets at all costs. The first thing came to her mind was to visit the house where the masked men had been hold-ing their ritual.

***

An open for inspection sign was placed in front of the red brick house. The door was widely open. The real estate agent stood in the doorway of the mystic house. His freshly pressed white shirt with a burgundy tie and well-polished black shoes, gave him a professional look. He was meeting with potential clients.

Georgia approached him slowly." Is this house for rent?" She asked, pretending to be interested in renting a house.

"Yes, it's back on the market due to the home inspection." He an-swered.

"How do I find out who the landlord is?"

"Are you going to rent a house?"

"Yes, and I'd like to know the name and address of the landlord, please." She insisted.

"You can find your landlord's contact details in the tenancy agreement. Do you want me to put your name in potential tenants' list?" Asked the real estate agent as he opened the folder.

Georgia felt numbness and tingling in her hands. She had puzzled look on her face. "I'd like to inspect the house first to make sure that everything is in order, "she found an excuse to get herself out of an awkward situation.

The moment she entered the house, she felt underlying tension. There was too much negative energy around her. She could feel it in her heart, chest and even on her skin. She rushed into the small room where she had seen the masked men performing their ritual. The room was empty. Georgia heard the sound of quick footsteps in the hallway. The potential tenants were walking up and down the stairs.

She watched them with curious eyes. The real estate agent offered a tour of the house to new visitors. Georgia took a chance to escape. She couldn't get a clue about where to start looking for the hunch-back.

Chapter Eight

It was Oscar's birthday. He turned ten years old. "Happy Birthday to you! Exclaimed Georgia as she gave the dog a toy bone. Oscar jumped up on her bed, he licked her face, neck and ears and dragged her up to a sitting position. He almost bathed her face to show his gratitude and affection to her. Georgia took a lazy step into the kitchen. Oscar went to find a safe place to hide his toy.

Georgia's dad was sitting at the breakfast table. He was reading a newspaper while drinking black coffee. "Where is the birthday boy? Why is he so quiet?" He asked.

"Oscar must be busy with his new toy," replied Georgia and grabbed a bottle of milk from the fridge. She poured the milk and a cup of cereal into the bowl. Tucking her feet up, she made herself comfortable on the padded chair. She stared at the print on the organic cereal box, squinting her eyes. Daniel glanced at his daughter sidelong. "Improve your posture, dear. Sit up with your back straight, please. Proper posture will help your muscles work better." He said.

Georgia straightened her shoulders. He smiled at her and looked through the surfing news headline. "Dear, have you heard about the Aussie surfer who survived the shark bite yesterday?" Daniel showed her the shark attack surviving surfer's front-page photo.

"Hmm, he must be very lucky." She replied.

"Oh, yes. The shark tossed the surfer from his board. He was bitten on the leg. The surfer punched him while climbing back on his board. Fortunately, he managed to escape."

"I guess a life-threatening accident makes you view life from an absolutely different perspective."

"You are right, my dear." Daniel put the newspaper on the wooden table, which had deep scratches from cutting bread on it. "Hey, I almost forgot to ask you, have you prepared the speech for your graduation ceremony?"

"I'm working on it. Speaking in front of the large audience at drama school makes me feel overwhelmed."

"Emotional honesty, that's what audience needs," said Daniel, waving his index finger in the air.

"Thank you, Dad for your advice. I will take it into consideration," replied Georgia and poured fresh water into the bowel for the dog.

Oscar entered the kitchen shaking his tail happily. Daniel petted him on the shoulder, "Today I'm going to introduce him to my friend's dog," he said and scrunched the dog's back.

"Perfect idea! Doggy date is the best!" Exclaimed Georgia.

Daniel put the dog on a leash and took him out for a walk. Georgia spent the whole day writing her graduation speech. She was trying to choose the right words. As soon as she started listening to her heart more than her head, the words came naturally to her.

The graduation ceremony started with exciting live music performance. The graduate students were filled with Joy. They were celebrating the beginning of a new chapter in their lives. Georgia was a little bit saddened. Saying goodbye to her favourite teachers and friends wasn't easy for her. She went up on the stage to give a speech to the audience. The warmth in her smile drew audience to her. Her speech was short and emotional: "Thank you all for letting me be a part of the family. I've been lucky to have teachers who helped me identify my strengths and weaknesses. The workshops allowed me to find my unique point of view that is influenced by my believes and comes from me and no one else. Thanks for creative freedom, you allowed me to do things without fear. I have grown as a person professionally and personally within these walls. Thank you," she said and bowed slightly.

The audience gave her a big round of applause. Her speech left a lasting impression on everyone. Daniel captured magical moments on his camera. He was touched, his eyelashes were wet from tears.

"We are very proud of your achievement, dear." Said Daniel. He stumbled over his words as he was too excited.

"And, I'm very proud to have parents like you. Thank you so much for your support." She replied.

"Have fun at your party, sweetie," said Maria and lovingly kissed her daughter on the forehead.

Georgia's parents linked arms as they went outside. Georgia joined her friends.

The graduation ceremony was followed by a party. The huge table was loaded with exquisite home-cooked dishes made by the graduate Students.

Georgia received many compliments on the chicken stew dish. One pot meal consisted of seared chicken pieces cooked in tomato sauce and herbs. She also had prepared another dish for the special occasion. It was made of minced meat and rice seasoned with oregano, onions and mint. All wrapped in fresh, crunchy grape leaves. Georgia enjoyed tasting food created by her fellow classmates. She discovered different ingredients, seasonings and cuisines. She complimented her friends for their efforts. Most of all, she loved Indian dish, butter chicken made by her friend, Payal.

"Your dish tastes as good as it looks," Georgia said to her.

"Thank you, I think my dish looks similar to your chicken stew." Replied Payal.

The girls chuckled softly and exchanged their recipes.

After dinner, Georgia and her friends hit the dance floor. They danced the night away, celebrating the unforgettable time spent together. Georgia wanted to share her emotions with her best friend, Linda. She called her on the phone, but Linda didn't pick her call.

It was after midnight, by the time she returned home. The bubbles in champagne made her tipsy. She needed rest to sober up. She drew her blanket up against her neck and went to sleep.

Georgia woke up with a migraine attack. Pulsing pain began in the forehead and around the eyes. She drank a cup of very strong coffee to ease the pain. She was concerned that Linda didn't call her back, so she called her friend again to find out how she was doing. Linda answered her call right away.

"Hi, Linda, would it kill you to call me back? I was worried about you." Georgia said in an irritated tone.

"Sorry about that. I've been so busy, I totally forgot to call you." Linda apologised to her.

"Are you okay?" Georgia asked.

"Actually, I'm little bit confused. What's going on with you and Morgan? Can you please explain it to me?" She asked.

Linda's response perplexed her. Georgia got distracted and upset. Her headache gradually got worse; the pain shifted from the forehead to the back of the head. "How he dared to talk to you behind my back?" She asked in a strict tone.

"Dear, I know you are a very nice person, but Morgan is also my friend and he isn't so bad either."

"Listen, Linda, he is angry with me because I refused to sleep with him. He threatened me once that he would ruin my reputation and I see, he has already started his dirty game."

"Okay, Georgia, let's talk later. I have to go now, take care." Said Linda and ended the conversation.

Georgia was saddened and frustrated. She realised that she has lost her best friend because of Morgan. It pained her to think that she would never have a chance to become Linda's child's godmother. She stepped into a cold shower as she needed to cool down a bit. Her feet touched the ceramic floor, it was so cold that she curled her toes. Georgia couldn't stop seeing Morgan's face through her mind's eye. His face was red with anger, his eyes looked mad, steam was coming out of his ears. Georgia turned on the cold-water tap, the chill water raining down from the shower, helped her to escape Morgan's malicious gaze. It made her feel empowered and in control. She felt energised, her painful headache has almost gone.

***

It was a cloudy autumn day. The sun was playing hide and seek, as if the weather couldn't make up its mind to give a little sunshine or not to give. Georgia hurried out to meet the fortune teller. As she reached the park, she saw Otto sitting on the same bench they shared last time. He was looking through his phone. Georgia took a step towards him. The tree branch leaves shaking sound made her startled. She jumped with alarm like a frightened baby deer. Georgia glanced behind the oak tree, but there was nobody there. She noticed a bird taking a flight from the branch of the tree and breathed a sigh of relief. "Hi, Otto, how are you doing?" She shouted to him from a distance.

Otto smiled and waved at her. Georgia sat on the bench next to him. "Let's pick up where we left off. I can't wait to hear all about my past, present and future." She said.

Otto rolled wooden prayer beads through his hand. He took a deep breath and said: " I saw a bright light while meditating. I learnt many things about you."

"How did you get that power?" Georgia was curious.

"Well, It's in my genes. My grandfather was a tarot card reader. He taught me everything."

"What did you learn about me?" Georgia interrupted him.

"You are a kind hearted person, very strong. You help yourself to overcome the challenges in your life. Your weakness is being naïve. You trust people easily."

"Please, tell me something about my past," she looked at him with questioning eyes.

"I think you broke up with someone you love. Don't worry, soon you will meet a person who will rock your world," he stared at her, knowing with certainty that she was eager to learn more.

Georgia gave a sigh of melancholy.

"I see tension in your facial muscles. You are restless, you need a freedom from anxiety. Open up to me, trust me." Said Otto.

Georgia opened her heart to him. She immediately told him about the incident with the hunchback. Her mouth felt dry as she spoke. Otto listened patiently; his eyes were calm. " I need to ask the universe questions through meditation. Once I get a clear answer, I will get back to you," he said and rolled his beads again. "If you want to have a piece of mind you need to forget about the incident, that's my advice."

The weather turned cold. Georgia lifted her hands to her mouth and blew on them to keep them warm.

"Let's call it a day. You are getting cold." Said Otto.

"Sure, I hope to see you soon." She replied.

The trees swayed by the wind; Georgia got startled again and jumped off the bench. She was afraid not to bump into the hunchback.

"Are you all right? " Otto asked.

"I'll be all right when I find out why I'm being chased." She said. There was a hint of hesitation in her voice. "I don't want to live in a constant state of fear anymore. I'd like to live like a normal person," Georgia sighed deeply.

"Don't worry, you will get an answer to all your questions soon." He said.

Otto escorted her home, he made sure that she was safe. After talking with him, Georgia became confused. One part of her mind was asking her to stop thinking about those who did her harm, but the other part kept insisting on seeking revenge. Georgia put herself a task to learn more about Morgan and his circle of friends. She called her friend, Romina as she was Morgan's distant relative. Romina suggested meeting over lunch at sea food restaurant.

***

Georgia stood outside the restaurant, waiting for Romina. It started raining and in the blink of the eye, the rain turned into hail. Georgia found the shade to protect herself from getting wet. She watched crystal balls falling from the sky, wide-eyed. She stretched her arm to catch golf ball-sized hailstones.

Romina came by cab. She climbed out of the car, covering her head with a handbag. Hailstorm almost smashed the cab. Romina looked frightened. She was terrified by loud thunder. Georgia grabbed her arm and led her into the restaurant. They took the table facing the ocean. The dark, big waves were roaring up the beach. Romina removed her white leather jacket and draped it over the back of the chair.

"Are you all right?" Georgia asked.

"Honestly, I've been better." She replied with a bitter smile.

The waiter greeted the ladies politely. He poured the water in their glasses and handed each of them a menu. They ordered a sea food platter and a bottle of red wine. Romina shook the rain from her hair. "What bad weather we are having! I've never seen such big hail-stones. Honestly, I hate walking in the rain. I feel annoyed when a single drop of water falls on me." She said with an irritated tone.

Georgia sighed deeply. "Please, stop being grumpy, Romina. We do complain so much when homeless people are struggling in rain. It's very hard for them to find a shelter and stay out of wet. When the rain stops, they come across another problem. It's very difficult for them to dry their clothes. I've heard a lot of heartbreaking stories about the poor people who get sick just because they can't change out of their damp shoes. In the heavy rain street dogs also suffer a lot. I know that in some countries, street dogs can't find a shelter easily. They hide under the cars and buses to escape the rain, which is very dangerous for them." She said with sadness in her eyes.

Romina blushed with shame. "I will never ever complain about rain, I promise." She said a little guiltily.

Georgia gave her a tight-lipped smile. "By the way, I wanted to talk to you about Morgan."

Romina felt uncomfortable, her breath quickened. "If you want to get to know him better, why don't you talk to him?"

"Well, I tried to talk to him, but in vain. He is playing hot and cold with me. I really don't want to end a friendship with him," said Georgia, pretending to be interested in fixing things with him.

"I think he is disappointed in you." Replied Romina after a long pause.

"Morgan is too impulsive, I guess; he is acting without forethought. I'd like to talk to him in person, but he isn't answering my calls." Said Georgia.

Romina eyed her doubtfully, she didn't know what to say, therefore she tried to change the subject. "Dear, you look different today. I think you have put on some weight."

Georgia looked at her with a frown on her face.

The waiter brought a huge seafood platter of oysters, smoked salmon, clams and prawns. It was served with Marie Rose sauce.

"Yum!' Romina exclaimed, licking her lips. She slurped down the oyster from the liquid filled shell and swallowed it.

Georgia didn't feel like eating. She grabbed a piece of salmon from the platter, but didn't touch it. Her mind was busy with disturbing thoughts.

Romina broke the silence: "Dear, why aren't you eating?"

Georgia promptly helped herself to a piece of salmon. "Hey, did Morgan talk to you about me?" She asked.

"I will give you a friendly advice," said Romina with her mouth full. "Distance yourself from Morgan's circle of friends. Time will settle everything."

Georgia was persistent. "Romina, could you please give me Morgan's home address? I will really appreciate your help," she said looking at her pleadingly.

"You are so stubborn," said Romina. She tore a page out of her pocket notebook and wrote Morgan's home address on it. "I hope you will clear the air with him, get rid of all doubts and negative feelings," she said as she handed her a piece of paper.

Georgia gave her a satisfied look. Romina finished eating her lunch and went to the restroom. Georgia called the waiter to fetch her some water.

"Would you like anything else?" He asked.

"Check, please." She replied.

Georgia thanked the waiter for the delicious lunch, paid the bill and went to the restroom. Romina was fixing her makeup.

"I'm afraid I have to leave now. Please, don't worry about the bill." Said Georgia.

"Thank you, dear. You have a nice personality and I'm sure you will solve misunderstandings," said Romina as she squeezed a pimple on her nose.

"I hope so. Thanks for giving me your time." Replied Georgia.

Morgan's house was facing the beach. Georgia climbed the fence to get into his front yard. She rang the doorbell, but nobody answered, then she pounded on the door. Finally, Morgan appeared in the doorway. He seemed to have just woken up. His hair looked untidy.

He was barefoot and wearing just his blue underwear. "What are you doing here?" He asked as he rubbed his eyes, wondering if he were still asleep or awake.

"Hi, Morgan," she said calmly, trying to be friendly.

Morgan didn't reply. Peering into the hallway, Georgia saw the empty beer bottles on the floor. "Listen, we need to talk." She said.

"I don't have anything to discuss with you. I told you everything you needed to hear, but it seems to me that you quickly forgot it." He said through glittered teeth.

"I'm not going to take much of your time, just tell me who is the hunchback and what does he want from me?" Her voice was rising, though she tried to control it.

"Stop the bullshit! You are just bluffing; you've caused me a headache." he said and slammed the door shut in her face.

Georgia knocked on the door a few times. Morgan got annoyed. He opened the door sharply; his eyes were glowing with anger. Georgia gave him a stern look. "I warn you, if you bother me again, I will unmask you and reveal the truth." She shouted at him. Her heart was beating so loudly, she knew he could hear it.

Morgan laughed nervously. His laugh sounded like a maniacal laughter straight out of a horror movie. "You are getting on my nerves. Do whatever you like. You can't prove anything, you don't have any evidence," he said as he kept laughing nastily.

"You don't have any humanity left in you. We are done here." She said and left.

Morgan was right, Georgia didn't have any evidence against him, so she decided to surrender her will to the will of God. She knew that God was working while she was waiting…

***

Fresh aroma after rain was very pleasing. Georgia inhaled the powerful scent of damp soil. She stuck her tongue out and tasted water droplets falling from the trees. Her favourite park was quiet and empty. Georgia was eagerly waiting for the fortune teller, who promised her to get her questions answered. Her eyes searched toward the spot she had last seen him. Taking a step forward, she espied him in the far distance. Otto was sitting on newspapers on a rain -soaked bench under the oak tree. He was picking his nose with his left index finger. He noticed her coming in his direction and quickly pulled his finger out of his nose. Otto blushed with shame when he was caught in an awkward moment. Georgia greeted him cheerfully. "How are you doing, Otto?"

"I think I've got nasal polyps." He said shyly.

"Well, you need to see a doctor; he might prescribe a nasal spray to reduce irritation. By the way, steam inhalation may help. My grandfather used to try the fastest way to shrink nasal polyps at home. He had been inhaling steam from boiled water." Said Georgia.

"Thanks, I will keep it in mind. Hey, are you going to talk standing up? Please, sit down," said Otto as he scooted over on the bench.

"I don't like wet buttocks." She chuckled.

"It's best to be at the same eye-level," Otto stood up and stretched. He put his mobile phone on the bench. "While meditating I saw a man, it must be him with whom you had a conflict. He likes you; he doesn't have bad intentions in his heart." He said reassuringly. In a split second, Otto got interrupted by a ringing phone.

Georgia instinctively glanced down at Otto's phone screen. She saw Morgan's name and number on the display. She went rigid with shock. She realised it was a set-up, it seemed that Otto was just a pawn in Morgan's game.

Georgia gave him a furious glare. Otto's face turned pale as she caught him in a lie. He quickly grabbed his phone from the bench and put it in the pocket. "Do you have any questions?" He asked, avoiding her gaze. Otto looked confused. He was so distracted by an incoming phone call that he stumbled over the bench.

Georgia arched her eyebrows at him. She tried hard not to lose her temper. She hesitated for a moment, then said: "Finally, I've got an answer to my question."

"Please, let me know if you need anything else. I genuinely want to help you, I'm honest with you." Otto's eyes were shifty.

After a long, uncomfortable silence, Georgia said: "You must first be honest with yourself. I know that Morgan asked you to trick me into believing that you were my well-wisher. Shame on you."

Otto shrunk before her; he became smaller in size. Georgia looked into his eyes and realised that there was no use to get upset on him. His eyes were empty, absolutely empty... She looked at him with a touch of pity in her eyes. Otto looked away; he was unable to bear her glance.

Georgia took a shortcut home. Her heart was heavy. She quickly undressed and slid into bed. She stared at herself in the mirror. A large, square shaped mirror was hung on the wall in front of her bed.

She had a look of devastation on her face. Emotional exhaustion sneaked up on her. Georgia couldn't sleep peacefully. She saw a dream that made her terrified.

Georgia dreamed that she walked barefoot down the empty street. She heard a high-pitched whistling sound coming from behind. Turning around, she saw eternities' greatest enemy, the Devil following her.

He was wearing a black hooded cloak. His face was covered with a black metal mask. Georgia could see his eyes through small holes cut

into the mask. His evil eyes blazed like fire. Georgia had a panic attack. Her heart jumped into her stomach with fear. She felt weakness
in her legs. Her eyes misted over as hot tears ran down her cheeks.
She used the last drop of energy and ran. She cried in pain and terror.
The Devil gave her a roar of rage and ran after her. The shiver of fear
passed through her shoulders; her back trembled. Georgia fell down in
her haste. For a split second, she thought she was dying. Reaching
down her shirt, she took out a gold cross necklace. She held the cross
pendant up towards him. It was shining so bright that the light came in
the darkness. The Devil couldn't bear seeing the holy cross pendant,
he let out a miserable scream and turned to dust...

The dream was so vivid, Georgia screamed in her sleep. She woke
up sweating and shaking with emotions. Maria heard her daughter's
scream and rushed into her room. "What happened to you, sweetie?"
She asked in a frightened voice, seeking to find out the cause of her
distress.

Georgia was fighting to hold back tears; her throat felt a bit swollen. Maria gave her a tight hug. "Tell me what is bothering you,
dear?" She asked as she sat on the edge of the bed.

"I had a nightmare." She said and two fat tears fell from her eyes.

"Calm down, breathe, it's just a bad dream." Said Maria.

"How can I calm down? Oh, Mom, my life turned upside down,"
said Georgia in an arguing voice. "Everything I've ever loved and
cared about is gone, my boyfriend, my friends, Mr. Thompson's
film... I just lost trust in people. What did I do to deserve this?" Her
nose was chapped from sobbing.

"Please, don't say that. You are very lucky. God gave you a key to
unlock his blessings. You need to follow God's plan patiently and find
your happiness. You are born under the Aries zodiac sign. You are a
warrior, my dear. You don't fear anything, you have guts to fight."

Maria's words had a positive impact on her. She felt so much better inside. The worry gradually lifted from her mind. Georgia wiped
tears with her hand and said: "I need to figure out my birth chart. It

can deliver important messages to me about my personality, relation-ship, career. I have so many questions."

"What could it hurt, "said Maria.

Surfing the internet, she found an astrology website. She sent an email to the astrologer and got a prompt reply from him. Georgia gave the astrologer her birth details to create her natal chart and made face to face appointment with him.

Chapter Nine

The astrologer lived in the suburb. Georgia arrived exactly at the scheduled time. She saw a sign on the door saying: 'please, leave your shoes outside.' She quickly removed her running shoes and neatly tucked her socks into them. The front door was slightly open. Georgia entered the house barefoot, she walked through the narrow corridor in search of the living room. The astrologer was sitting at the desk, his nose buried in the book.

Georgia coughed softly to attract his attention. The astrologer smiled at her warmly. He was an old man with a white beard and moustache. He was wearing a loose white shirt and white pants. His costume was accessorised with a long red scarf, made of fine silk. Georgia perched herself on the edge of the floral print sofa. She looked pleadingly into his eyes, expecting him to rescue her. Georgia told him her story. Her voice was a little bit strained; her hands were trembling. The astrologer listened to her attentively. He heard tears in her voice. He printed out her detailed natal chart. It was a snapshot of the sky at the very moment she was born. "Georgia, you are pure in heart. You are capable of resisting evil influences." He said.

Georgia stared down at the piece of paper; she was eager to find a clue to her soul's purpose. The astrologer ran his fingers through his long beard and said: "You will have to go through a rough patch. You will face a lot of challenges on your road. Faith in God will help you overcome obstacles in life. With God's hand of protection no one can touch you. Those who cause harm to you will be reversed and the evil will be sent back to them."

"But why do I have enemies?" She asked sincerely.

The astrologer closed his eyes, as if he were trying to get in touch with his inner self. "Your real enemy is the Devil. He is jealous because God has blessed you with a gift of pure heart. The Devil has thousands of faces. If you meet mean people in life, simply ignore them. They are possessed by the evil spirit. Let go of anger and forgive everybody. Start a war not with them, but with the Devil."

Georgia felt the truth in his words. She was filled with a sense of awe. "I believe I can win the spiritual battle. I'm not afraid of the Devil anymore." She said with confidence.

"That's the spirit!" Exclaimed the astrologer. "Forget about all the reasons why you can't make your dream a reality. There is one rule you need to obey; you should think positively to attract positive energy. Believe in yourself, work hard and you will earn respect, power and love."

His words made her calm. She had a feeling the heavy load was lifted off her shoulders. She restored her self-confidence. "Thank you for giving me hope. Before coming here, I've been sad and miserable. I think God sent you into my life to help me with getting through tough times," she said and smiled with her eyes.

Georgia walked out of the astrologer's house filled with hope. She paused a moment at the black iron gate and took a deep breath. Closing her eyes, she murmured to herself: "I choose to forgive those who hurt me." Her mind instantly sent a positive signal to her heart...

***

After several days of rain, the sun finally appeared. Georgia opened the window wide and exclaimed: "Dear Sun, you were missed!" The amazing rays of sun streamed into her bedroom and made her smile. The smile on her face got even bigger when she received an unexpected text message from her favourite artist, Sebastian. He wanted her to visit his art studio urgently. Georgia was greatly delighted. It took her only a few minutes to get ready.

The moment she entered the studio, her face became gloomy. The walls were empty, white sheets were draped over furniture. Sadness lingered in the atmosphere. "What happened, sir?" She asked in a worried tone.

"Tonight I'm leaving for Spain, my dear." He replied.

"Really? Is everything all right?" Georgia looked in his eyes, as if she were trying to read his mind.

"I have longing to reunite with my love, Rebecca. As you know, my heart has melted," he said, smiling. "I don't hold grudge against Rebecca anymore. I managed to overcome my ego and forgive her."

"I see you followed your heart," said Georgia and gave him a big, happy smile.

"Well, I'm still in love with Rebecca. Thank you for opening my eyes to the truth and my heart to love."

His words made her cry. Black mascara tears slid down her cheeks. "I'm happy for you, but the fear of losing you makes me feel a little bit melancholy," she said, still crying.

"Everything will be okay, dear. You won't lose me. I will keep in touch with you."

"Do you promise me?" She asked.

"Pinkie swear." He replied.

They both locked their pinkie fingers together to signify that a promise was made.

"Actually, I have a surprise for you," said Sebastian and handed her a card board tube.

"What is it?"

"Open it."

Georgia popped out the plastic cap and from inside very carefully pulled a rolled canvas. It was a portrait of herself. Georgia's face lit up when she saw it. Sebastian took her arm in a fatherly way. "This portrait represents your soul, your spiritual connection with the divine. It belongs to you." He said.

Georgia's head spun with excitement. "Thank you for everything, sir. I will remember you every time I look at the painting. I can't wait to hang it up in my apartment." She said looking up at him with shy, grateful eyes.

"You are welcome, I'm pleased to see you happy." He said.

Georgia glanced down at a big brown suitcase, leaning against the wall. "Can I accompany you to the airport?" She asked pleadingly.

"No, I don't like saying goodbye," he said, gently caressing her hair.

"Well, I guess, I'll take off now. Have a safe journey, maestro!" Said Georgia and kissed him on the cheek.

"Never change, my friend. Stay as incredible as you are. You are wise beyond your years, dear. You are the young woman with an old soul." He said with a trace of smugness in his voice.

She gave him a bear hug and made a gesture of farewell. Georgia rushed home, holding the card board tube close to her heart.

She gathered her parents together in the dining room and showed them the portrait of herself. "Isn't it amazing?!" She exclaimed. Her eyes sparkled while gazing at the painting.

"It's a masterpiece. Said Daniel.

"We should hang this beautiful painting above the piano." Suggested Maria.

"I agree." Replied Georgia.

"We have to choose the best frame for the artwork." Said Daniel.

"I want a simple frame, preferably in white." Said Georgia decidedly.

Daniel straight away went to the frame shop and got the canvas framed. When Georgia saw it, a radiant smile spread across her face. Daniel hung the painting above the piano. It made the room brighter and lighter.

Georgia was so excited that she didn't want to leave the dining room. She lay down on the sofa, looking at the painting in admiration. She wanted to jump into the painting and make the world inside come alive. Georgia closed her eyes and went to sleep immediately. She had a pleasant and joyful dream.

Georgia dreamed that she was wearing a traditional Indian costume- Saree. It was held on her waist with the jewelled belt. Gold bangles jangled on both of her wrists. Her hair was tied in a bun knot adored with flowers. She had a red dot on the centre of her forehead. Her hands and feet were painted in red powder. Around her ankles she wore bells that made a rhythmic sound as she danced on the stage. Her parents were sitting in the front raw, watching her spectacular dance performance. She danced gracefully with great charisma. Her performance was very emotional and moving. She received a standing ovation from the audience.

Georgia woke up from a sweet dream with a smile on her face. "Maybe the universe is trying to tell me something?" She thought out loud.

A bright idea flashed into her mind. She opened her laptop and began looking for the Bollywood film studios. Georgia sent her portfolio, showreel and curriculum vitae to the casting directors, in attempt to get a casting call. She stepped out to the balcony and looked up at the sky with hopeful eyes. After a couple of hours, Georgia checked her electronic mailbox.

To her great surprise, she was selected for an acting audition. Georgia nearly fell of a chair as she read the email. It seemed that the universe granted her wish. She rushed into the kitchen, holding the open laptop in her hands. "Mom, I think I hit the jackpot! She exclaimed.

"What made you so happy today, dear?" Maria asked.

"I'm going to India," she said and showed her mother the email she received.

"Hooray! Congratulations! You have my full support," said Maria in a delighted voice.

After breakfast, Georgia and her mother cheerfully went to the travel agency to purchase a flight ticket. The travel agent named Sonya was Maria's friend. Sonya jumped up from the chair with excitement as she saw Maria and Georgia entering her office. She greeted them with a big smile and open arms.

Sonya had a shag haircut. Her hair was layered to various lengths. The layers made the hair full around the crown. Her hairstyle looked very rock 'n' roll. She was wearing the seventies midi dress and vintage brown shoes. Maria looked her over from head to toe. "You are looking younger and younger every time I see you," she complimented her friend.

"Likewise, you and Georgia look like sisters. The resemblance is striking," she replied with a British accent and chuckled softly.

The travel office was warm and inviting with modernised furniture. There were photos of different countries on light blue walls. Sonya's desk was full of souvenirs. Georgia liked the small carvings of the Egyptian pyramids. Sonya spun the desk globe around and asked Georgia. "Which country are you going to visit?"

Georgia stopped the round globe with her index finger pointing to India.

"Great choice, I'm sure travelling to India for the first time will be unforgettable for you." Said Sonya.

She provided Georgia with important information about her trip, flight schedules and accommodation options.

"Thank you so much, I appreciate your help." Said Georgia.

"Welcome, my dear. You are so pretty and smart, I'm sure you make boys go crazy for you." Sonya chuckled.

"Honestly, I'm focused on my acting career. I think relationships will distract me from achieving my goals," said Georgia, gazing at the desk globe.

"Good on you. I'm in my late fifties. I'm single and never had a boyfriend." Said Sonya.

Georgia looked at her in shocked silence.

"Call me old fashioned, but I never wanted to have sex before marriage. I was in love once. He wanted to have a love affair with me, but I rejected him. I always wanted to lose my virginity on a wedding night." She said with a sigh.

"Oh, Sonya, you are still young. You have plenty of time ahead to fall in love." Georgia said promisingly.

Sonya smiled with her eyes. "You are a very kind girl, Georgia. I wish you a safe journey and good luck! I'm pretty confident that you will fulfil all your dreams," said Sonya as she handed flight tickets to her.

"Touch wood!" Exclaimed Maria. She rapped her knuckles on the wooden desk three times to distract evil spirits and request good luck.

Before travelling to India, Georgia took some time to learn basic Hindi phrases. She wanted to get to know Hindi cinema better. Every day she watched five Bollywood movies in one stretch. She took online classes to expand her vocabulary. Georgia was an enthusiastic learner, she wanted to put her knowledge into practise. She decided to communicate with people of Indian origin and overcome a language barrier.

She asked for assistance from her Indian friend, Payal. It turned out that Payal was overseas. Unfortunately, Georgia had nobody else to talk to in Hindi.

***

The wind howled through open balcony door. Georgia slowly got up from bed and pushed the door shut. She accidently overheard a conversation between a man and a woman in Hindi. The voices were coming from the apartment next door. After a few minutes, she heard the sound of footsteps outside her front door. Georgia peered through the heart shaped spy hole. She saw an Indian man and a woman standing in front of the elevator entrance. It seemed that an Indian couple have just moved in next door. Georgia's eyes brightened with an idea. She quickly put on her clothes and stepped into the floor area. Georgia wanted to introduce herself to her new neighbours. They were talking to each other so fast that she couldn't manage to jump into their conversation. The woman was wearing dark brown baggy pants, tapered at the ankle and a loose grey shirt. She had long hair down to her thighs. A single thick braid made her look very attractive. The long beard man was wearing a piece of material wound around his head. His pink headpiece looked stunning. The woman adjusted the collar of his shirt. She planted a kiss on his cheek and stepped into her unit. The man pressed the elevator call button.

Georgia took a chance and entered the elevator in attempt to start a conversation with him in Hindi language. She knew that keeping silent in the elevator would be a missed opportunity for her, so she greeted him in Hindi: "Hello! My name is Georgia. I'm your next-door neighbour."

He smiled and tilted his head side to side. "Nice to meet you. I'm Rasheed."

The elevator stopped on the ground floor. He stood back and motioned her to exit first. "Do you speak Hindi?" He asked as they walked out of the building.

"I'm learning. I would love to become fluent in Hindi." She replied.

"That's very good." He said.

"Thank you, Rasheed Ji."

He looked at her in surprise. "I see you are aware of the etiquette of Indian culture. You didn't forget to add 'Ji' at the end of my name as an expression of respect.

Receiving praise made her feel more confident. "Which way are you heading?" She used new Hindi words into a sentence and managed to ask him a question.

"I'm going to the train station."

"Oh, I'm also heading that way," she found an excuse to continue the conversation with him.

The apartment building was about ten minutes' walk to the train station. Georgia had enough time to practise Hindi speaking. "I like your headpiece." She said.

"Thanks, it's called Turban. It's a sign of purity, it represents my faith." He said proudly.

"Does the colour of the turban mean anything?" She asked.

"Well, colours like white, orange and blue are traditionally used during religious celebrations. Red is worn during weddings. I have more than fifteen turbans with different shapes and colours. Every day I match the colour of the turban with my outfit."

"I'm sure your pink turban will brighten up a day for your co-workers," said Georgia. "I'm sorry if I made grammar mistakes while speaking in Hindi."

Rasheed smiled and ran his long fingers through his beard. "Actually, your Hindi isn't bad. You must be a fast learner."

"I'm glad to hear that," said Georgia. "Do you wear a turban at home?" She kept asking questions.

"No, I keep my head covered when I'm in public." He replied.

Reaching the train station, Rasheed pulled the train ticket out of his pocket. Georgia gave him a demure smile.

"I really enjoyed talking to you, it's such a pity there is no more time to talk." She said.

Rasheed smiled. "Have a great day." He replied.

Georgia headed home, repeating newly learned words and phrases in Hindi. She was filled with satisfaction that she used her time productively. When she reached her apartment building, she noticed a guy sitting in a squatting position in front of the closed entrance door. He was gazing at Georgia through squinting eyes. As soon as he stood up and smiled at her, she recognised him. It was Sam, her ex-boyfriend. He looked totally different. Sam was thinner, pale and depressed. His head was shaved completely bald. He was smoking a cigarette.

"Hey, Georgia. It's been a long time since we last met. I felt terrible after breaking up with you." He said, chewing on his fingernail.

Georgia looked confused. "I think we have already said enough." She replied shortly.

Sam finished his cigarette and lit another with a silver lighter. He clicked his lower jaw forward and blew smoke rings, shaping his cheeks and lips, as if he were sucking an ice lolly.

"I've never seen you smoking a cigarette. You are a dentist; don't you know that smoking can cause gum disease and tooth decay?!"

"I'm going to quit smoking. I know it's a bad habit," his voice was raspy from cigarettes.

"You better do this. Smoking is very harmful for your health."

"Babe, let's sit in my car and talk for five minutes, please," he said and glanced at her with begging eyes.

Sam looked so desperate, for a moment she felt sorrow for him. The car smelled of cigarette smoke. It made Georgia dizzy, she rolled down the window to get rid of the smell. Sam grabbed her hand and squeezed it tightly. "I missed you," he said and seemed to mean it. He leaned towards her and kissed her on the lips.

Georgia was emotionless. She didn't feel anything when he kissed her. She didn't feel those butterflies anymore. Sam couldn't make her want him. She twisted her head back to avoid his lips. "The spark between us is gone. I'm sorry, Sam," said Georgia.

"Babe, we can get it back."

"Please, forget about me and move on."

"I will prove to you how much I've changed. My love for you is real."

Georgia closed her eyes in annoyance. "I'm sorry, but I don't feel the same connection with you that I used to have."

"Just give me a second chance, that's all I'm asking for. What we had was so special, I don't want to end things and pull the plug." He said in a sad voice.

Georgia didn't say anything. She had a total blank expression on her face. She hopped out of the car and closed the door without looking at him.

Stepping into her apartment, she heard cooing and fasting sounds coming from the bathroom. Maria was giving the dog a bath. "Georgia, where did you disappear? I need your help; Oscar resists me and tries to escape the bathtub," she said and handed her a pitcher to fill it with warm water.

"Oh, I know, he doesn't like taking a bath."

Oscar got excited to see Georgia, he started splashing around in a tub of water. Accidently, his foot slipped, he lost traction and got very scared. Georgia gave him a treat to calm him down." Good boy!" She motivated her four-legged friend.

She scooped up warm water with a pitcher and poured it over his back. She kept doing it until the dog's body was completely wet. Maria applied tearless shampoo around his head using a sponge. "Sweetie, please pour some water over the dog's head gently." She said.

Georgia stood still for a moment. Her mind was occupied with Sam. She realised that she didn't love him anymore. She didn't have the urge to hang out with him. When he kissed her, she felt that she wasn't sexually attracted to him. Sam was just a stranger to her.

"Sweetie, your mind is somewhere else, are you okay?" Maria asked.

"Oh, sorry," replied Georgia and poured warm water over the dog's head.

Oscar didn't like getting his head wet. He looked up at Georgia with very sad eyes. After a bath, Maria towelled down the dog and rewarded him with another treat for good behaviour. Oscar seemed proud of himself.

"Oh, Mom, I have good news, I totally forgot to share. I got acquainted with our Indian neighbour. I met him in the elevator. I'm so happy to have a chance to improve my Hindi speaking." Said Georgia.

"Good for you! I think the elevator journey is a perfect opportunity to meet new people and make new friends. Next time you meet him write down the new words in your pocket notebook. You will begin to recognise new words when you read. It will give you the confidence to learn even more words. Trust me, if you follow my advice, you will develop a rich vocabulary, dear." Said Maria.

"Yeah, It's so true. Simply talking with him helps me discover new words. I guess, I need to use new phrases frequently in conversations to memorize them quickly and easily."

"I'm very proud of you, sweetheart. Keep up the hard work," she said and looked at her fondly.

Georgia planned on meeting Rasheed again. In the morning, she tiptoed over to the front door and put her eye to the spyhole. As soon as her Indian neighbour appeared in front of the elevator, she rushed out the door.

"Good morning!" He greeted her in Hindi.

"Hello, Rasheed Ji. We keep bumping into each other." She said with a giggle.

There was an awkward silence in the elevator. Rasheed was fiddling with his smartphone. Georgia initiated the conversation. "I see today you chose to wear the black turban; it looks classy."

"Thank you. The black turban is very practical and versatile. It goes with any outfit." He said, looking down at his smartphone.

Georgia accompanied him to the train station. She didn't stop talking. Rasheed glanced at his wristwatch.

"Oh, I think I might be late for work. My alarm clock went off and I couldn't wake up on time," he said as he quickened his step.

"All right then, I won't take your time anymore. Have a positive day at work." Said Georgia.

"Thank you very much." He replied.

Georgia sat on the bench in front of the train station. She put the pocket notebook on her lap and added the new words to her vocabulary. She was already thinking about the next topic to discuss with her Indian neighbour…

Georgia's plan worked. Her Hindi has been improved a lot. Everything was fine, until she met Rasheed again. Georgia quickly entered the elevator. Rasheed looked a little bit confused. "Oh, I forgot my glasses at home. Please, don't wait for me. I'll take the next ride." He said.

Georgia decided to wait for him outside the apartment building. A few minutes later, Rasheed appeared. When he saw her, he got somewhat vexed. Georgia felt his tension. "Are you all right?" She asked.

"To be frank with you, my wife is a little bit concerned. She believes I'm cheating on her." He said with a sigh.

"Oh, I'm so sorry to hear that. Did you give her any reason to doubt your feelings for her?" She asked, genuinely being interested in the issue.

"Actually, she thinks I'm flirting with you." Said Rasheed. His eyes were clouded with concern.

Georgia went red in face from embarrassment. "But what made her think so?"

"My wife saw us walking down the street a couple of times. I told her that you and I kept bumping into each other coincidently, but she didn't believe me. I love her and I don't want to hurt her feelings. Please, don't get me wrong, I'm at an awkward position. It's better if we avoid each other." Said Rasheed.

"I understand, you don't have to worry about it. I will talk to your wife and explain everything." She said with honest concern.

Georgia made an apology basket for Rasheed's wife. She filled it with fruits, gourmet snacks and treats. She visited her Indian neighbours in the evening. Rasheed's wife opened the door.

"Hi, I'm Georgia. Can I come in for a few minutes? I'd like to talk to you."

"Okay." She replied and guided her to the living room.

Rasheed was sitting in an armchair, watching TV. He turned the TV off as he saw her. Georgia gave the basket to Rasheed's wife and sat down on the front edge of the sofa.

"Thank you," said the hostess and placed the basket on the round table.

"You are more than welcome. I'd like to apologise for any inconvenience I've caused. The thing is, I'm going to travel to India for a movie audition. I just wanted to practise Hindi speaking, that's why I kept Rasheed engaged in conversation. I'm truly sorry if I upset you." Georgia said apologetically.

Rasheed's wife got relieved. "Koi baat nehi." (It's okay.) She said in Hindi and smiled. "My name is Bhairavi."

"Such a beautiful name." Said Georgia.

"Thank you." She replied.

"All right, I better go now. I don't want to bother you."

"Please, stay. I have just prepared popular Indian desert, rice pudding. You should try it." Said Bhairavi.

"Oh, sweets are my weakness. I will definitely stay." She replied and leaned back on the sofa.

Bhairavi went to the kitchen. Rasheed smiled at Georgia. "Thank you for your kind gesture, you are a very nice person." He said.

Georgia blushed when he complimented her. Bhairavi brought three small white bowls filled with cardamon spiced Indian rice on a tray. She sat the tray down on the table and handed a bowl to Georgia.

"The flavour of this pudding is yummy. It's so creamy and gentle," said Georgia, inhaling the aroma of the rice pudding.

"I'm happy you are enjoying it." Said Bhairavi.

"My wife has golden hands." Said Rasheed proudly.

"Where did you guys meet?" Georgia asked.

"Actually, our parents took an active role and played matchmakers for us. It was a team work between parents and us." Replied Rasheed.

Bhairavi offered Georgia a cup of Indian tea and said: "When my father asked me to meet Rasheed, I didn't hesitate. Parents always know what is best for us."

"Oh, I see, you made a right choice as you are happily married now," said Georgia as she put her hands around the mug of hot tea.

"Yes, it was the best decision I've ever made." Said Bhairavi.

Rasheed looked at his wife with love and longing. "I let my parents find someone for me on one condition: If I didn't like the girl, I wouldn't marry her. I like a blend of tradition and modern independence that gives us a chance to find perfect matches. When I first saw Bhairavi, I knew she would be my life partner." Said Rasheed confidently. Bahriavi blushed with pleasure.

"Actually, my wife couldn't speak Hindi well. We lived in different states and spoke in different dialects." Rasheed continued telling his story.

"No way!" Exclaimed Georgia. "Did you teach your wife Hindi?" She asked.

"Yes, I did. I think it doesn't matter if a married couple doesn't speak the same language, the main thing is to listen to each other's heart." Replied Rasheed.

Bhairavi chuckled. "Thanks to my husband, my Hindi is good now, so I can give you free Hindi lessons if you like." She said to Georgia.

"I appreciate your concern. I would love that, but I'm leaving for Mumbai tomorrow evening. I'm blessed to have such good neighbours." Said Georgia.

Chapter Ten

At last, the departure day has come. Stepping into the airport, Georgia's heart started racing. She approached the ticket counter to check in her luggage. Once she received the boarding pass, she rushed to the terminal store and bought some toffees with nuts.

The passengers gathered in the waiting area before boarding the flight. Georgia felt carefree and happy. She observed people to kill the time. She watched them very carefully, without letting them know. She wanted to learn their body language and facial expressions, but their faces were buried in their cell phones. It seemed that social networks kept them busy. Ripping open the bag of chocolates, she took a bite out of the salted caramel toffee. Georgia distinctly heard someone say 'hello', she turned her face and saw a little girl with a cute pigtail coming towards her. She was holding a fairy tale book in her hands. As she approached Georgia, she sneezed into the crook of her bent elbow. "Excuse me." She apologised.

"God bless you." Said Georgia.

"Thanks. Where did you get the toffee?" She asked in a wobbly voice.

"I bought it from the chocolate shop," replied Georgia and grinned at her. A small piece of chocolate was stuck in her teeth.

The girl tucked the book under her arm. She put her tiny hand in her pocket and pulled out the twenty-cent coin. "Can I buy a toffee for twenty cents?" She asked.

"I'm afraid you can't buy anything with twenty cents." Replied Georgia.

The little girl frowned. "Then why does the twenty-cent coin exist?" She asked.

Georgia laughed out loud. "Even though it's a small amount, it's your money. If you start saving money in the piggy bank, you will notice that a little will become a lot quickly," she said and handed her a toffee." Take it, dear. it's yummy."

"Thank you," replied the girl. She grabbed the toffee and ran back to her mother, who was busy reading a newspaper.

An hour passed. The passengers started boarding the flight. Georgia found her aisle seat in the exit raw.

A chubby man in his sixties, with red cheeks and double chin sat in the window seat next to her. "Could you please wake me up when food is served?" He asked, adjusting his seat belt.

"Sure, no problem," replied Georgia and smiled politely.

The chubby man popped off his shoes, made himself comfortable and fell asleep even before all the passengers have boarded.

When the flight attendant served food to passengers, Georgia woke the chubby man up as she promised him. He yawned out loud. "Thank you for waking me up, I'm so hungry," he said as he placed his tuna sandwich and salad on the tray table.

"You are welcome," she replied.

Georgia didn't like airplane food, she only had tea and biscuits. The chubby man wiped his mouth on his shirtsleeve. "Why are food serving sizes so tiny? He complained as he finished eating his sandwich.

"Actually, I didn't eat my sandwich. You can have it if you like," said Georgia and handed him a wrapped sandwich.

"Thanks," he answered and swallowed the second tuna sandwich in one piece. When he finished eating, he went back to sleep.

Georgia's eyelids were heavy as she was sleepy. She moved her seat back and put her sleep mask on, but her peacefulness got disturbed by the chubby man's snoring. She put her ear plugs in her ears and tried to get some sleep.

A few minutes later, the chubby man tapped her on the shoulder. "I need to go to the toilet." He said.

Georgia stood up slowly and moved to let him pass by. By the time he returned, Georgia was already sound asleep. She was tapped on her shoulder again. "Sorry, I need to go back to my seat," said the chubby man and raised his eyebrows at her.

Georgia stood up, stretched and yawned. Once she settled back in her seat, she covered herself with the blanket and closed her eyes. The silence didn't last long. The chubby man woke up screaming at the top of his lungs.

Georgia got so scared that she pulled the blanket over her head. He looked at her with wide open eyes. "Sorry, I dreamed of being in a plane crash." He apologised.

Georgia peered out of the blanket. "It's okay," she said and handed him a bottle of water.

The chubby man drank a water bottle in one sip. Georgia breathed deeply to settle her nerves. She gave up trying to sleep.

Meanwhile, morning has arrived. The flight attendant offered Georgia a hot hand towel. She pressed it to her face and freshened up. When the plane got lower, she asked the chubby man to pull up the window shade as she wanted to get a good view of the landscape from above.

"You can't see very much of the landscape, it's covered in clouds," he said, looking at her with a serious expression.

Georgia didn't say a word, she knew that arguing with him was totally pointless. The pilot landed safely. The passengers clapped their hands in excitement. Georgia thanked God for a safe flight as she made the sign of the cross.

On the arrival at the airport, Georgia went through the passport control. She waited impatiently in a queue. She felt absolutely exhausted after a sleepless night. Georgia was already at the front of the line when someone tapped on her arm. She was so fatigued, she almost fell. She turned her head and saw the chubby man. "Sorry, I'm in a hurry. Can I stand in front of you?" He asked.

Without saying a word, Georgia stepped back and found herself standing last in a long queue. She almost fell asleep standing up. After the passport control, she collected her bag from the luggage carousel and wheeled it to the taxi rank area.

Stepping out of the airport, Georgia felt an unusual heat. The pavement was so hot that her shoes couldn't protect her feet well enough from burning. She had a feeling she was walking barefoot. Georgia noticed a tall man with a bushy moustache holding up a card with her name on it. She smiled and waved at him. The man smiled back in a friendly way.

"Welcome, ma'am! I'm at your disposal. The film director asked me to take you to the house where you will be staying," he said and walked her to the car.

"Nice to meet you," said Georgia as she shook hands with him.

The driver put her bag in the boot of his car. Georgia made herself comfortable in the back seat and fell asleep immediately.

An hour later, the driver woke her up, patting her lightly on the shoulder. "Ma'am, we have arrived." He said.

Georgia rubbed her eyes to acclimate them to the day. She stepped out of the car, looking around curiously.

"Ma'am, I hope you will enjoy your stay here," said the driver and guided her to the grey house, surrounded by tall green trees.

"Such a nice place!" Georgia exclaimed and quickened her step.

As she approached the house, she noticed an Indian pariah dog lying next to the cardboard box. The light brown dog looked up at her with kind eyes. She came closer to the dog and to her great joy, she saw the adorable puppies crawling out of the box. Georgia counted eight pups. They looked different from each other. Puppy siblings had different ear floppiness, coat lengths and different sizes. The mother dog felt that Georgia wouldn't hurt her puppies, so she let her pet them.

"Ma'am, you are lucky, the mother dog trusted you with her puppies. She wouldn't let anyone touch them." He said.

Georgia giggled happily.

The green gate creaked loudly as the driver opened it for her. A middle-aged woman with a yellow scarf on her head, stood in front of the house. She greeted Georgia solemnly. "Hello, my name is Alia. I will clean and cook for you, so you can relax." She said.

"Thank you so much, Alia. I appreciate your help."

Alia walked her upstairs to her room. The room had wooden walls. Georgia threw herself faced down on the king-sized bed. She buried her face in a large, soft pillow. All she could feel was her own happiness.

Georgia woke up at dawn to an unusual noise. She thought that a coppersmith was striking metal with a hammer. Stretching her arms and legs, she jumped off the bed. Georgia opened the window and looked out curiously. To her great astonishment, she saw two green birds sitting on the window sill. They were making rhythmic metallic sounds. 'Tuk-Tuk!' The little birds with bright red heads looked adorable. They leaned forward, shook their wings intermittently and flew away. Georgia laughed in delight. She ran down the stairs, humming a tune to herself.

Alia was preparing breakfast for her. "Good morning, ma'am. You seem to be in a good mood," she said with a smile.

"I slept like a baby last night and woke up to the birds singing."

"Oh, I guess, the coppersmith barbets visited you and made you smile." Replied Alia.

"They are just amazing. Their colour, size, sound, actions, all are so cute," said Georgia, her eyes brightened with excitement.

Alia smiled at her. "Do you want me to call the driver to take you to the Film studio?" She asked.

"Oh, no, I would like to take a rickshaw ride for the first time." Replied Georgia.

Alia poured some milk in her bowl. Georgia sipped hot milk and smiled with pleasure. "This is the best milk I've ever tried," she said, licking her top lip.

"I know, cow's milk tastes great." She replied.

Georgia asked Alia to pour some milk in a bowl for the puppies. Alia reached into the cupboard and pulled out a large aluminium bowel. "Feeding homeless dogs is a kind gesture," she said and handed her the bowel filled with milk.

Georgia put the bowel in front of the cardboard box. Happy puppies lapped up milk in a blink of an eye. The mother dog observed them from a distance. Georgia lovingly caressed her smooth head. Even though she couldn't say the words, her eyes expressed sincere gratitude.

Georgia headed to the local market which was close to her house. She inhaled the scent of exotic spices; the smell evoked a pleasant emotion. She saw a woman carrying a basket full of bananas on her head. Georgia approached her, smiling. She held a lady finger banana up to her nose and smelled the sweet aroma. She bought a hand of bananas.

"May God bless you," said the banana seller with a slight bow.

Georgia thanked her in Hindi and peeled off the skin of banana. She took a big bite off fully ripe fruit. It was so sweet and tasty; she ate five bananas at once.

Georgia walked slowly along the narrow road. She saw a three-wheeled motorised vehicle known as rickshaw coming towards her. She jumped in and gave the driver the address of the Bollywood Film studio. The driver opened a bottle of water and poured it into his open mouth. He drove off at high speed. Georgia felt like she was on a roller coaster ride, her hair blowing in the wind. She felt free, the blood pumped through her veins. Adrenaline gave her muscles more oxygen and made her feel good. She screamed with excitement. The rickshaw driver laughed in a hearty manner and drove faster and faster.

Georgia was in high spirits as she arrived at the Bollywood film studio. The director was waiting for her in the audition room. He was a pleasant looking, middle aged man. "Hello, Georgia, my name is Avinaj. I hope you are enjoying your time in India," He gave her a genuine smile.

"Namaste, Avinaj Ji," replied Georgia, pressed her hands together in prayer and bowed her head.

"Please, make yourself right at home." He said.

Georgia sat down on the green velvet sofa and put her knees modestly together.

"If you are ready, you can start reading your monologue," said the director as he put his eyeglasses on.

Georgia closed her eyes and took a deep breath. In her mind's eye she saw a golden light circling her head.

The light gave her a power and confidence. Georgia began to read the dramatic monologue. She had a very vivid emotional flashback. She recalled every ounce of pain she had ever felt, every rock that had been thrown at her and produced real tears. Georgia put her rage and sadness into the scene and released emotions stuck in her body. She expressed her character's true feelings.

When she finished reading the monologue, Avinaj Ji stood up from the chair and exclaimed: "I found my heroine!"

Georgia's cheeks blushed red. "Thank you, sir." She said.

"Tomorrow we will hold a press conference to announce our upcoming film." He said and took off his glasses. He wiped them on a handkerchief, outside and in.

"I will fulfil my responsibilities to perfection." She said. Her eyes were shining with excitement.

Georgia walked out of the audition room and lightly slid down the banister. Reaching the house, she heard sounds of Indian music coming from the kitchen. She slightly opened the kitchen door and saw Alia dancing; she was rocking her wide hips side to side. Alia noticed Georgia staring at her and immediately stopped dancing. "Ma'am, can I help you with anything?" She asked, looking embarrassed.

"Can you teach me belly dance?" Georgia asked.

Alia smiled modestly. "I'm just a self-taught dancer."

"Don't be shy, your dance was very elegant and vibrant."

"Thank you very much, ma'am. Dancing makes me really happy, besides it helps me to burn some calories and be in good shape."

"Stop calling me ma'am, please. Call me Georgia," she said as she pumped up the volume of music and kicked off her shoes. "Let's get started, shall we? Show me what you've got."

"The most important rule for a dancer is to feel music, you shouldn't be afraid to have a little fun." Said Alia. She created a dance routine for Georgia. "You need to talk with your hands, every movement is symbolic," explained Alia to her very clearly and raised her heavily braceleted arms.

Georgia quickly memorised new dance moves. She danced with artistic power and truly enjoyed herself.

After dance class, she asked Alia to take her to the shopping mall as she wanted to buy some presents for her parents.

The mother dog and her puppies escorted them to the auto rickshaw stand. Georgia and Alia hopped into one of the rickshaws.

"Alia, look at the dogs they are still following us," said Georgia. Her tone was startled and amused.

"I guess, the dogs are grateful to you. They sense you are a nice person," said Alia.

It took the Auto-rikshaw driver ten minutes to reach the shopping centre. Upon entering the building, Georgia and Alia went through a quick metal detector scan.

"Do you want to get yourself something cool?" Alia asked.

"Sure." She replied.

"I think writing your name on rice grain would be a perfect idea as rice art is considered to bring good luck." Said Alia and took her to the rice writer.

A man wearing an orange turban greeted Georgia in Hindi. He started writing the name on the single rice grain with a very fine-tipped technical drawing pen. Once the rice writing was completed, he placed the rice grain inside a small glass. In a couple of minutes, the personalised keychain was ready.

"That's the coolest keychain I've ever seen!" Exclaimed Georgia.

She came across many beautiful souvenirs. Georgia chose a gift for her father that matched his personality. She bought a hand carved phant sculpture for him. She knew it would be a fine addition to his travel souvenir collection. She also bought herbal shampoos and hair oils for her mother.

"Thank you, Alia, I'm grateful to you for your help. Shopping task is ticked off my list."

"My pleasure, Georgia," she said and gave her a tight-lipped smile.

Georgia woke up the next day to the first ray of the sun. She was full of energy, ready to tackle the day. Alia accompanied her to the film studio. They walked up the marble stairs to the function room. The special guests were waiting for Georgia. Everyone was curious to see the heroine of the film. As soon as she entered the function room, the reporters circled her, pressing their microphones toward her face.

"Thank you for the warm welcome. It's an honour for me to work with Avinaj Ji. I will put my heart and soul in this project." She said in Hindi.

The reporter interrupted her speech and asked her a question: "Ma'am, where did you learn Hindi?"

"Oh, I'm self-taught. I will learn Hindi fluently, I promise." She answered.

"It's going to be your debut, are you nervous?" Another reporter asked her.

"I'm not nervous. It's my future, it's something to look forward to, not to fear." She replied.

The interview went successfully. Georgia held herself confidently.

After the press conference, the director approached her: "Thank you, Georgia. You made me so proud. We will start working on our project in a month."

"I should be thankful to you for giving me a wonderful opportunity. I had the most unforgettable experience in my life." She said.

Chapter Eleven

Georgia had a pleasant flight back home. Arriving at the airport, she rushed to the baggage hall. She noticed her medium- sized brown bag rotating around the baggage claim carousel. Georgia leaned down, trying to reach for it, but in the blink of an eye, someone lifted her bag off the carrousel. She looked up and saw a very handsome young man. He was wearing a black hood over his baseball cap. "Hello, senorita. So good to see you. Do you remember our photoshoot on the fancy yacht?" He asked, smiling.

Georgia arched her eyebrows in surprise. "Joe! She exclaimed. "It's been ages since I saw you." She had never been so happy in her life to see anyone.

Joe eagerly took a step forward to hug her.

"How are you?" He asked.

"I'm doing great. I had a trip to incredible India. Where are you coming from?"

"I was in Italy, visiting my parents. Seeing you put me in a good mood." Said Joe.

"How is your fiancée?" Georgia asked. She felt herself blushing.

"Actually, we broke up. Tara had jealousy issues. Trust me, jealousy in relationship is a nightmare for everyone involved." He admitted.

"I'm sorry to hear that." Said Georgia.

"Hey, what are you doing tomorrow? I'd like to invite you to a concert of a famous Italian singer. It would be great if you join me."

"Why not?! I love Italian songs. Thank you, Joe." She blushed again.

"Perfect! It was so good running into you," he said and kissed her on the cheek.

It gave her happy goosebumps...

Georgia took a cab home. Her mind was occupied with pleasant thoughts. Joe put a continuous smile on her face. He appeared out of nowhere and swept her off her feet. Good vibes transmitted by his presence made her feel uplifted. She was drawn to the powerful positive energy sent through his eyes. Feeling her inner happiness, she smiled into her heart. Georgia opened the front door to her apartment and noticed the 'Welcome home' card on the hallway wall.

"Let's pop the champagne"! Exclaimed her father. The champagne cork soared through the air and made it rain bubbles.

Georgia laughed heartily. She hugged her father and relaxed in his arms.

"It's my turn now," said Maria, pulling her daughter gently towards her.

Oscar barked with excitement. He squeezed the upper part of his nose between their legs. Georgia's father raised a glass and made a toast: "I'm so proud of you, my dear. You worked hard to make your dream a reality. What more could I ask for?! Keep up the good work, kiddo," he said with dampness in his eyes. Daniel emptied the glass of cold champagne and kissed her on the head.

Georgia felt overwhelmed by positive emotions. She went to her room to get some rest and recover from jet lag. After only a week away, the room seemed slightly less familiar to her. It looked a bit bare. Her clothes were folded in the bureau drawer neatly. The translucent curtains were replaced with linen white roman blinds.

Georgia noticed an envelope lying on the bedside table. She quickly opened it and let out a cry of joy. She was so happy to hear from her dearest friend, Sebastian. The artist was planning to take his wife, Rebecca on a world cruise. Georgia was delighted that after so many years, the pair were reunited at last.

She was extremely impressed with Sebastian's handwriting. She showed the letter to her mother. "I'm amazed by the magnificent calligraphy."

"Wow! His handwriting looks majestic. It's just a work of art." Said Maria admiringly.

"His nickname should be – A Master Penman," Georgia said, giggling. "My handwriting is just horrible; I'm embarrassed about it. It's not even eligible."

"Honey, don't feel bad, the main thing is to write your heart out. Let your friend know how important he is to you." Replied Maria.

Georgia tried her best to write neatly. She expressed her gratitude for his love and concern and shared her memorable travel experience with him. She wished Sebastian a safe and happy vacation.

The next morning, Georgia ran down the street to the nearest post office. "Hello, sir, I'd like an envelope and a stamp, please," she said to the clerk.

"Sure, what delivery options do you prefer?" He asked.

"I want the fastest way to mail a letter, please."

"All right, no problem. Nowadays people seldom pick up a pen and paper to write a letter and express their feelings." Said the clerk with a smile.

"Well, to my mind, a hand- written letter is very important. When I write a letter, my mind is totally focused on the content and I'm carefully thinking about what I'm writing."

"I agree, I text my brother every day, though we are not exactly opening up to each other." He said.

"Yeah, text messaging keeps us connected, however, a hand-written letter is more personal. It gives us a chance to connect to each other on a deeper level." She replied as she put the letter in the envelope.

***

Georgia met Joe at the front entrance of the concert hall. She had a big smile on her face.

"You look beautiful, senorita." Said Joe.

"You are handsome yourself." She returned the compliment.

A lot of dressed up Italians were gathered in a hall. They were talking loudly and very fast in their native language. Georgia and Joe sat in the front raw. He gently wrapped his arm around her shoulder. When he touched her, she felt electric spark. She slowly drew Joe's arm more closely to her. His nearness and warmth comforted her. Georgia wanted to stay in his arms forever.

The curtains raised and the Italian singer appeared on the stage holding the guitar in his hands. The audience started clapping to express admiration. The singer's strong, powerful voice touched the very depth of Georgia's soul...

During intermission Georgia and Joe visited the backstage area to meet an orchestra performer, who was Joe's close friend. He was having a rest in the dressing room.

"Hello, Roberto," Joe greeted his friend.

"Hi, mate. So good to see you," he said and shook hands with him.

"This is Georgia," Joe introduced her to him.

"Hello, sister," said Roberto and gave her two kisses. First on the right cheek and second on the left cheek.

"Thanks for such a lovely concert, I'm really enjoying it." She said.

"I'm glad to hear that." He replied.

Joe reached into his pocket and pulled out his golden pocket watch. He opened the cover of the watch with a small button in the crown. "Oh, the intermission is almost over. We will get out of your hair now." He said to his friend.

"See you later, enjoy your evening." Replied Roberto.

The light dimmed in the lobby. They returned to their seats. Georgia wanted to feel the warmth of his embrace again, so she put her head on his shoulder. Joe lightly touched her cheek.

The Italian singer turned his audience into performers. He asked a bunch of audience members to get up on stage with him. They began dancing and singing together.

"Brava! Bravissimo!" Joe was shouting loudly.

"Wow! What a performance. Thank you for inviting me." Said Georgia.

"You are welcome, senorita." He said, kissing her hand.

After the concert, they took a short walk to get some fresh air. "Hey, let's have dinner at the Italian restaurant. What do you say?" Joe asked her.

"Sure, who don't like Italian pizza," She said giggling.

Joe held her in his arms, caressing her back. It made her feel warm and safe. He lifted her dimpled chin and gazed into her eyes. "Can I ask you a question?" Joe whispered in her ear.

"Shoot." Replied Georgia.

"May I kiss you?" Joe's voice was full of affection.

"Yes, you may." She replied shyly.

They closed their eyes and kissed under the romantic lighting of an old-fashioned street lamp.

As they walked into the restaurant, he said proudly: "Welcome to little Italy."

The atmosphere was lovely, the air was filled with the smell of fresh tomatoes, garlic and cheese. Georgia breathed in the aroma of the Italian food and sat down in a soft cushion seat.

A man in a black suit took his violin and began playing an Italian folk song. Georgia tapped her feet in time to the music. "It feels cosy, almost like home," she said, bouncing in the chair.

"I knew you would love this place." He replied firmly.

A waiter brought a bottle of Italian wine. He poured a small amount in the glasses and waited for them to taste it. He glanced at Joe and asked: "Chef, do you want to try today's special?"

Georgia was wide-eyed with astonishment." Wait a minute, are you a chef?" She asked him.

"Oh, yes. I'm a Chef. I totally forgot to tell you, senorita."

Georgia shook her head and sighed; "You never fail to amaze me."
They ordered 'Quattro formaggi,' the four-cheese pizza.

"I'd like to hear your story," said Georgia and looked at him with curious eyes.

"Well, I'm an Italian guy. I was born in Rome; my parents still live there. I resemble my mother in character, my father- in appearance. My passion for cooking has been inspired since my childhood. My mother is an excellent cook, I inherited secret recipes from her. She encouraged me to become a chef."

"Is modelling your hobby? Georgia sked. "You looked natural in front of the camera."

"Oh, no, I'm not interested in modelling. The photographer was having lunch with his colleagues at my restaurant. He introduced himself and promptly offered me a modelling job, the photo shoot on the fancy yacht. As I'm fond of yachts, I immediately accepted his offer. I guess, It was the best thing I've ever done, because I met you. See, fate brought us back together."

Georgia's eyes sparkled. Joe took a sip of the wine and said: "Hey, do you know what is the best way to get to know each other in a very short time?"

"Could you please enlighten me?" She smiled at him gently.

"It's very simple. Friendship is based on trust and honesty. Let's share our secrets with each other. Are you in or not?"

"Okay, I'm ready." She said.

"Tell me one thing you don't want me to know."

She paused for a moment, then gave a long sigh: "Well, I have been chased by men who were involved in a secret practise of satanic worship," said Georgia as she turned pale. "The mystery isn't solved yet. Actually, I still don't know why they chose me as a target."

"Oh, how did you meet those people?" He asked in a perplexed tone.

"I accidently appeared in the wrong place," said Georgia with regret in her voice. "That's the long and the short of it."

"Did you report an incident to the police?" He asked, genuinely concerned.

"Not yet, there is no evidence, no witness. I can't prove anything right now, but I hope sooner or later the truth will come out."

"I will be by your side any time you need me," said Joe and held her hand.

"Thank you, Joe. Now it's your turn to tell me your secret."

Joe scratched his head. "When I was a teenager, I was a drug addict. I have been suffering for nearly six years. It really destroyed me. I am ashamed of the life I used to live. My friends had really bad influence on me. My parents supported me during hard time. They advised me to join group therapy class. It helped me a lot as I could express my feelings in front of others without being judged. Finally, I managed to overcome drug addiction. I have a feeling I have been reborn." Said Joe.

"Thank you for your honesty, Joe. It takes courage to admit your mistakes."

"You are a gem person, senorita. You just don't listen to words; you carefully listen to the emotions."

Joe pulled out his pocket watch and glanced at it. "You know, I have fear of passing time. I want time to slow down a bit. Life moves very fast; I'm scared I won't have enough time to fulfil all my dreams. Before I die, I want to do something meaningful and leave my mark behind."

"I love your pocket watch; it looks so unique." Said Georgia.

"It belonged to my grandfather. The watch has his initials on its cover. I inherited it from my grandpa on his death. When I have a son, I will give it to him." He said and chuckled softly.

Georgia felt emotional attraction towards him. She realised that she was attracted not just to his body, but also his mind and heart. Joe leaned forward to kiss her on the mouth, but the waiter spoiled the moment. He brought an extra-large pizza and placed it on the wooden table.

"Ooh la la!" Exclaimed Georgia and put a slice of pizza on her plate.

The four-cheese pizza looked so delicious; it made her mouth water. "Italians are masters of pizzas, I will have a muffin top on my tummy tomorrow," said Georgia.

They burst out laughing. Joe asked the musician to play the love song on the violin. Then he stood up and asked Georgia to dance with him. She accepted his invitation with a graceful bow. They made a strong connection on the dance floor, harmoniously moving together. He kissed her tenderly on the lips. Joe inhaled her breath, felt the warmth of her perfumed skin, tasted her strawberry lipstick. Georgia felt vulnerable, she got lost in kissing…She was absolutely sure that Joe was her soul mate. He entered her heart, like it was a place he always belonged…

Georgia got home with a smile on her face. The taste of his kiss remained on her lips. She still felt his warm embrace. A phone call from an unknow number snapped her from thoughts. She got startled to hear her ex- boyfriend's voice. Sam asked her to go on a date with him. Georgia wanted him to let go of hope of getting back together, so she agreed to talk to him in person. She suggested to meet at the coffee shop the next day.

***

Georgia opened the window and discovered a bird's nest on outside her window sill. "Welcome, little sparrow!" She Exclaimed and rushed to her mother's room to tell her the exciting news. "Mom, I'm so thrilled. The swallow made a nest outside my window."

"Oh dear, that's great," said Maria and went to see it with her own eyes.

"I'm so lucky to get a chance to be up close with nature." Said Georgia.

"Bird's nest is a lucky symbol, sweetie. It means that good karma will return to you for your good deeds."

Georgia giggled. "My swallow built a beautiful and cosy nest cup using mud. She worked so hard to build it. I hope soon this nest will be full of loud baby swallows." She said and laughed cheerfully.

The sound of birds chirping filled her with positive energy. Georgia gulped down fresh squeezed orange juice and went to the coffee shop to meet with Sam.

The atmosphere seemed boring and dull upon entering this time. Seeing him, she became a little sad. She felt awkward around Sam. He seemed pumped. "Babe, no kiss for me?' He asked with a cheeky smile.

Georgia gave him a kiss on the cheek.

"You look hot in tight yoga pants." He complimented her.

"Thank you, Sam. I'm planning to hit the gym today," she said and sat down in a chair opposite him.

"Would you like something to eat?" Sam asked.

"Just black coffee will be fine." She replied.

"You know, I quit smoking." He said proudly.

"Good on you! Stopping a bad habit immediately isn't easy."

"Actually, you motivated me to quit smoking."

Georgia blushed. She grabbed a coffee mug and took a sip. Sam took out a jewellery box from his jacket pocket. He opened up the small red box with an engagement ring. "Will you marry me?" He proposed to her with a tremble in his voice. Sam literary started shaking.

Georgia felt like the air was trapped in her chest. "Please, keep this ring for someone who will love you back," she said, her breathing was shallow. "I know, we have shared magical moments. Our first kiss blew my mind. It took just a second for the chemicals to produce in-love feeling, but now those crazy chemicals are not stimulated. Even though I felt passionate about you, my feelings for you faded away and disappeared. It seems we are not made for each other." She looked at him for a split second and lowered her gaze.

Sam looked devasted. "I know exactly when you lost interest in me. On the Valentine's day I made a mistake. I told you that I wasn't ready for a serious relationship. I deeply regret what I said. I want a fresh start, please, give me a second chance."

"I'm sorry, Sam but it's too late. My heart belongs to someone else. I hope we can still be friends." She said apologetically.

"No, Georgia, we can't be friends. Who is your boyfriend?" He asked, frowning eyebrows.

"He is the guy who touched my heart. Goodbye, Sam. I wish you all the best in life," she said and went out of the coffee shop with quick steps.

Georgia felt free as she opened up to Sam. She took a few deep breaths and headed down to the gym. Her pony tail was rhythmically bouncing behind her. Approaching the bus stop, she saw her old friends, Linda and Romina staring at her. Linda had a huge round belly. She seemed to have moved into the last month of her pregnancy. Georgia was very excited to see them. She even forgot that their friendship was broken and smiled happily at them. Linda ignored her. The look on her face was ice cold. She bent close to Romina and whispered something in her ear. They coldly turned their backs on her. Georgia's smile froze. Her body felt heavy, stress didn't allow her to move. Her feet were glued to the ground. Georgia felt like a wounded baby bird fallen from the nest. She felt lack of energy, so instead of going to the gym, she went back home. She realised that Linda and Romina didn't care about her, so she decided to let go of people who didn't appreciate her.

Georgia stuck her head out of the window and looked up at the bird's nest. She started communicating with the charming swallow. "My new friend, your presence makes me feel joyful. You fill me with warmth and love." She spoke slowly and clearly, as if she were talking to a small child. The swallow was chirping and singing. The sweet melody gave her motivation.

***

Georgia booked one-on-one boxing session with a personal trainer. She slipped into her white lycra top and black leggings and went to the gym with enthusiasm, humming a cheery tune. Entering the workout room, she greeted the trainer and put her red boxing gloves on. Georgia got ready to hit the punching bag. The trainer gave her instructions, trying to push her to her limits. "Slightly bend your knees." He said.

Throwing her first punch, she felt the sharp pain in the bones of her hand. "Ouch! That hurts," She exclaimed to express her pain.

"It's all right. Spin the punch fast, rotate your torso as much as possible and exhale as you throw the punch." Said the trainer.

Georgia took a deep breath and hit the heavy bag again. Her second punch was pretty weak.

"Listen to me, visualise a specific person who hurt you and attack him fast." The trainer kept encouraging her.

Georgia hesitated for a moment. Then she did exactly what he asked her to do. She closed her eyes and visualised herself hitting her worst enemy, the Devil in the face. Rage heated her blood as she punched the heavy bag very hard. She felt a bead of sweat between her breasts.

"Well done, boxing reveals a true fighter inside you." The trainer complimented her.

"Thank you." She replied and wiped sweat from her forehead with a towel.

Georgia felt light and good, she was filled with satisfaction. Her mind was busy analysing the boxing session when she fell down the stairs. She hit the back of her head hard on the floor and lost consciousness.

Georgia slowly opened her eyes and found herself lying in a hospital bed. Her parents were standing next to her bed staring at her with frightened eyes.

"I was worried about you, sweetie. Are you okay?" Maria asked her as she sat on the edge of the bed.

"What happened to me?" Georgia asked in a worried tone and put her hand behind her neck.

"Nothing serious, you had a mild head injury." Said her father.

"I have a severe headache and can't move my neck, but at least I'm still in the land of the living." She said and kissed her cross pendant.

"Apparently, someone pushed you down the stairs. He must be sick in the head. Please, don't worry, the police will collect evidence. You may be asked to make a statement today, dear." Said Daniel.

"Please, take plenty of rest and avoid stressful situations to recover faster," said Maria as she pulled the light weight blanket up to her neck.

Maria and Daniel went to the lobby cafe to grab a coffee. Georgia reached into her bag and pulled out her cell phone. She dialled Joe's number with trembling fingers. His voice overwhelmed her. She told him about her accident and started crying like a child. Joe was very concerned. He decided to make a surprise for Georgia and show her his affection and care.

Nearly one hour passed by. Georgia fell into light sleep. A knock on the door woke her up. She opened her eyes and saw Joe, poking his head into her room. "Senorita, may I come in?" He asked her in a low voice.

Georgia nodded her head and smiled broadly.

"I made an authentic Italian ice cream desert for you. I hope it brings joy to your day," he said and planted a kiss on her forehead.

"Oh, thank you so much for being so nice to me," said Georgia and glanced at him with love in her eyes.

Joe fixed the pillow under her head. He sat on the chair beside the bed and fed her an ice cream pie with a spoon.

"This is the best desert I've ever had." Said Georgia.

"It's because I put the key ingredient in it- my love," he said and looked at her the way she always wanted to be looked at.

Georgia was enjoying her ice cream pie when a nurse entered the room, followed by a police officer. There was an awkward pause. Joe stood up from his seat very quickly. "Senorita, I'm going to take off now. Please, let me know if there is anything I can do for you." He Said.

"Thanks for visiting me, keep in touch," replied Georgia and blew him a kiss.

Joe went out of the room and closed the door behind him with a click. The police officer walked towards Georgia with his leather file folder tucked neatly under his left arm. "Hello, Georgia. I hope you are doing well." He said and sat on the chair.

"Thank you, officer. I feel better."

"An eyewitness reported that she had seen someone pushing you down the stairs. She gave us all the details of the crime scene and a description of a suspect."

Georgia shrugged her shoulders. "Unfortunately, I don't remember anything," she said with a worried look on her face.

The police officer pulled the picture of the suspect out of his file folder and showed it to her. "Do you recognise this man?" He asked.

Georgia's heart rate became very slow. Her blood pressure dropped rapidly as she saw a picture of the hunchback. She fainted for a few seconds. The nurse asked the police officer to leave as Georgia was experiencing severe emotional stress.

At the time Georgia regained consciousness, she started crying. The nurse tried to calm her down. "You don't have to worry about a thing. You will give the statement to the police when you are ready."

"Hopefully my statement will help with the investigation," said Georgia as she wiped tears from her eyes with her hand.

As soon as Georgia's health condition improved, she was sent home from the hospital. Georgia was greeted by her dog in the hall-way; he jumped up on her and licked her face.

"Oscar was very sad. I guess he had an intuition you'd been in trouble." Said Georgia's father.

"I missed him so much," said Georgia as she squatted down to pet her four-legged family member. She hung her jacket in the hallway. Entering her room, she heard birds singing outside the window. Their songs brightened up her day. She opened the window and saw baby swallows; they popped their tiny heads from the nest in anticipation. They were naked, except for some grey feathers on their head and shoulders. They looked at her with black sparkly eyes. The birds seemed to be well fed and happy. Georgia laughed heartily. She sank into a chair by the window, enjoying the moment. Her peace of mind was disturbed by the phone call. The police officer needed her statement urgently. Georgia didn't waste time, she grabbed her jacket and rushed to the police station.

The police officer gave her a friendly smile. "Are you feeling better?" He asked.

"This time I won't faint, I promise." She said with a giggle.

"Please, take a seat," he said, pointing to a black leather chair.

Georgia sat down in front of him and hung her handbag over the chair. The officer started questioning her.

"Can you tell me what do you know about the suspect?"

"A while ago, I was invited to the house party organised by my friend, Morgan. I accidently saw the masked men performing in a satanic ritual in a secret room. I got scared and stormed out of the house. Since then, the hunchback has been chasing after me."

"Are you still in touch with Morgan?" He asked.

"No," she said and told him everything that she knew about him.

"Your life isn't in danger anymore. You have one problem out of the way. The hunchback was arrested on suspicion of attempted murder."

"But why? Why has he been obsessed with me?" Georgia asked innocently. She gazed into his eyes, wanting desperately to get the answer.

"He tuned out to be the member of the secret evil organisation. What I discovered was that he saw a high energy level of light coming out of your eyes. He admitted that your overpowering positive energy was more powerful than atomic bomb. I know it's weird, but he sees you as a threat. Don't worry about it, he won't do you any harm. He will rot in jail."

A cold sweat broke out on Georgia's forehead. The officer gave her a glass of water as he noticed that her hands were shaking. She drank a few sips of water and pulled herself together. "Is Morgan also arrested?" She asked, breathing heavily through her nose.

"Not yet, he has left the country."

Georgia signed her statement and left the police station. Everything looked good. The hunchback was finally arrested, but she felt totally drained, rather than elated. The emotional exhaustion built up and zapped her joy.

*****

Georgia invited her boyfriend to her place for dinner. She wanted to impress him with her culinary skills. She asked her mother to help her cook special dishes, following her grandmother's recipes.

"Mom, Joe is a professional chef. Freshness, flavour and quality are top priorities for him. We need to keep that in mind." Said Georgia.

"We'll try our best, dear. Hopefully he will be pleased with our dinner," replied Maria and winked at her.

They started baking a cheese pie. "Sweetie, if food is prepared with love, it tastes better. It's rather magical." Said Maria.

"I know, Joe says that love is a secret ingredient," said Georgia as she wiped her floury hands on her green kitchen apron.

The doorbell rang. Georgia removed her apron and ran to open the door. She greeted Joe with a big white smile and open arms. Joe looked very elegant in his black suit and tie. He handed her a bouquet of red roses. Georgia introduced her boyfriend to her parents and guided him to the dining room.

"Senorita, you look fantastic!" He exclaimed.

"You are really sweet. You always compliment me," she said, smiling.

"Are you feeling better?" He asked.

"Much better. You know, the police caught the man who pushed me down the stairs. He turned out to be a member of the evil organization."

"Jesus Christ!" Exclaimed Joe. "See, the truth come out sooner than you expected." He said and kissed her on the cheek. While embracing her, he accidently stepped on the dog's foot. The dog yelped in pain. "Oh, I'm so sorry, Oscar. I didn't see you enter the room," said Joe with a look of concern in his eyes.

The dog gave him a hard stare, with unblinking eyes.

"Oscar is overprotective. When someone comes near me, he gets jealous. He wants to take charge and keep me safe."

Joe squatted down and gently petted the dog behind the ears. "Oscar, I'm not your rival. We just fell in love with the same woman," he said and swung Georgia into giggling.

Georgia's father watched them through the glass door. He was happy to see his daughter smiling from the inside out. "Hey, Joe, do you have a little time to play a chess game with me?" Daniel asked as he entered the room.

"Oh, I'm not good at chess," he replied humbly.

Georgia tried to save her boyfriend from defeat. "I don't recommend you to play with my dad. He plays chess like a grandmaster." She said.

"Thank you for the heads-up, Georgia. I appreciate it." Replied Joe.

Daniel had a beaming smile on his face. "The fastest way to become a better chess player is to play often. The more you play, the more you improve your game. Come on Joe, don't be lazy," he insisted.

Joe could think of no other way than to say he would be happy to play. Daniel walked him into his study room. Joe sat down beside an antique carved chess board table.

"Are you ready for chess match?" Daniel asked.

"I will try my luck today. I used to practise chess puzzles when I was little."

"Don't worry, today you will learn the important chess strategy and tactics."

Daniel controlled the chess board from move one. Joe made a mistake in the beginning of the game. He started attacking too early and moved the same piece twice in the opening.

"Wait a minute my friend, you should always double check your moves. Never waste time memorizing opening." Said Daniel.

"I know that the main thing is to capture the king of the opponent," said Joe confidently.

"Oh, yeah. You need to make a threat while moving the pieces and limit your opponent's options." Daniel gave him an advice.

In between making moves they kept on chatting. "What do you like about my daughter?" Daniel asked him an awkward question.

Joe blushed a little. "Well, I can't find words to express my feelings fully. I just feel happy when I'm around her. I can be myself with her." He replied.

Daniel gave him a little smile. He seemed to be satisfied with his answer. As it was expected, Daniel won a chess game. He defeated his opponent without much effort.

"You are a champion! Today I learnt a lot from our game," said Joe and shook hands with Daniel.

"Thank you, Joe. It was a pleasure to play with you." He replied.

They came back to the dining room and sat around the table, covered with a white lace tablecloth. Georgia brought the baked cheese pie out of the oven. "Please, go ahead and start eating while it's hot." She said.

Joe was impressed to see the boat shaped pie with crusty ends. The pie was stuffed with melting cheese and topped with a raw egg and butter.

"The presentation of the dish is brilliant!" Exclaimed Joe.

"Break the ends off and mix up the egg, butter and cheese so that it almost becomes fondue." Said Georgia.

Joe took a bite of the cheese pie. "Super!" He exclaimed as he wiped his mouth with a napkin.

Georgia's father poured red wine in glasses. He raised a glass and gave a toast: "Cheers to true friendship!"

"Cheers!" Everyone said, clinking glasses together.

Maria handed another dish to Joe. "This is the red bean stew, beans are cooked and mashed with herbs and spices." She said.

Joe put two scoops of bean stew on his plate. "The herbs and spices are making this dish incredibly flavourful. Maria, could you please share the recipe you invented?" He asked in a respectful tone.

"Oh, I'm not going to give away my secret recipe," said Maria, laughing.

Georgia winked her eye at Joe. She leaned towards him and whispered in his ear. "Don't worry, I will steal the recipe from mom."

"I heard that!" Exclaimed Maria.

Everyone laughed loudly. After dinner, Joe asked her to play the piano for him. She gladly consented to do what he wished. Joe admired her playing the classical piano piece; he clapped his hands in appreciation. He pulled her closer in an embrace. "Is that a portrait of yourself?" He pointed to the painting hung proudly on the wall.

"Yes, this painting was made by a very talented Spanish artist."

"I love it. It shows your inner beauty."

Georgia was pleased that he got to the depths of the painting. They went to the balcony to get some fresh air. Joe stared into her eyes for a while before he leaned to give her a warm hug. "I'm going to Italy next week to finally attempt to start my own business. I'm planning to open a small restaurant in Rome."

"Wow! Good on you. I'm so proud of you." She exclaimed.

The night was full of stars. They were gazing at the sky. "Can you see the brightest star in the sky?" Joe asked.

"Yes, it's closer to the horizon." She replied.

"The bright star will follow you everywhere you go," said Joe and wrapped his arms around her waist.

Georgia had a feeling they touched each other's soul. Goosebumps rose on her arms. Joe took off his jacket and covered her up with it. He kissed her hungrily, as if he were trying to swallow her lips.

"I can't resist the temptation; your lips are so kissable." He whispered in her ear.

Georgia caressed his face tenderly.

"Senorita, it's getting late. I should go now before your parents kick me out of the apartment." Said Joe, smiling.

Georgia laughed at his words. "I will miss you," she said as she put her head on his shoulder.

"You will always be on my mind." He said.

Georgia escorted him out the door. Joe's car was parked on the opposite side of the road. Crossing the street, Georgia noticed her ex-boyfriend, Sam standing under the tree in front her apartment building. Georgia got perplexed. She didn't know what to do, so she decided to ignore him. She grabbed Joe's hand and calmly turned her back on her ex-boyfriend. Sam took a step forward towards them. "Babe, why are you ignoring me?" He asked, his voice was sarcastic. Sam behaved as if he and Georgia had never been partied.

A cold sweat poured down Georgia's face. Joe looked surprised. "Do you know this guy?" He asked, frowning his brows.

Sam didn't let her speak. "What's your problem, looser?" He shouted at Joe.

"Hey, man, are you looking for trouble?" Joe asked him rolling his eyes.

"I'm your trouble." Sam yelled.

"Please, don't pay attention to him, don't sink to his level." Georgia whispered in Joe's ear.

Sam displayed aggression towards Joe, as if it were a men's competition for a woman. He unexpectedly attacked him. Pushing joe's elbow down, he caught his head and got a handful of his hair. Joe got so furious that he broke Sam's nose with his head. His nose began to bleed. Georgia was crying desperately. "Please, stop, you are behaving like kids. I'm not a prize to fight over."

Sam wiped blood from his nose on his shirt. "Georgia is the most important person in my life. I won't give up on her easily," he said, breathing heavily.

"Are you crazy?" Joe exclaimed, making a circle motion of his finger at the side of his head.

"I'm in love with her. I even proposed to her. Our love story had its ups and downs. Georgia is my girl, do you understand?" He yelled at Joe.

Joe was green with anger. He turned to Georgia and asked her: "Is that true what he is saying?"

Georgia stood still, frozen with shock. She didn't say a word, just stared at him. Joe left without looking back. Georgia wanted to run after him, but she couldn't move her legs. Sam came up to her and put his leather jacket around her. "Babe, you must be cold." He said.

Georgia threw off his jacket in anger. "I thought you would have respected my feelings. You knew I had a boyfriend. Apparently, it wasn't discouraging for you," She said. Her eyes were watery as she held her tears back.

A soon as she opened the front door to her apartment, she bumped into her father. "Are you okay, sweetie? You don't look well." Said Daniel.

Excusing herself, Georgia rushed into the bathroom. She got on her knees, with her face close to the toilet bowl and threw up. Nervousness made her sick. Somewhere in her mind she thought Joe would lose trust in her. She washed her face with cold water, took a deep breath and walked out of the bathroom.

Daniel was waiting for her in the hallway. "Are you all right?" He asked, he seemed to be very concerned about his daughter.

"Yes, I'm fine. I just have an upset stomach," she replied.

"Oh, my poor baby girl, don't worry. Drink plenty of fluids, it will settle your stomach."

Georgia nodded her head. She looked worn-out. Daniel followed his daughter into her room. "Joe seems to be a nice guy. Do you know why I suggested a chess match?" He asked.

"I know, you missed playing chess."

"No, dear. I just wanted to test him. Playing chess helps me to read people. I wanted to know him better."

"Oh, really? How did you read his personality through a game of chess?" Georgia asked in surprise.

"I observed him through the whole game. I wasn't sure how would he adapt to certain scenario. How would he react to an early mistake. I wanted to see if he would immediately show signs of anger."

"Did he use swear words?"

"No, he didn't lose his temper. I was also interested to know whether he would let me win. I made a dumb move in the beginning of the game. Joe tried his hardest to beat me, he didn't let me win easily. I think Joe has good qualities. He is direct, honest, he has positive attitude and integrity."

"So, it means he passed the test, right?" She sighed.

"Yes, indeed." Said Daniel. "Get some sleep dear, tomorrow you will feel much better."

"Night- night!" Replied Georgia.

Daniel winked at her and closed the door behind him. Georgia felt restless. She called Joe but he didn't answer her call. She grew more anxious. She sent him a text message saying that she wanted to talk to him urgently. Joe didn't text her back. Having put on her pyjamas, she turned off the bedside lamp and slipped into bed, but she couldn't escape the waiting. She kept checking her phone every fifteen seconds. She got practically glued to it in the hope that he would finally call her. She started imagining the horrible things that might have happened to him. Georgia fell asleep after midnight with the phone in her hand.

She saw a dream that Joe was falling from a cliff. Georgia stood at the edge of the cliff. The fear of losing him gave her incredible strength and courage. Lying down with her armpits on the edge, she gave herself enough space to rear up and used her free arm to grab his hand. Georgia squeezed his hand so hard; she could see her purple veins through her skin. She managed to pull him out of the dangerous end safely. Joe looked at her tenderly, expressing his love through his glistening eyes. He wouldn't let go of her hand...

When Georgia woke up from her dream, she felt stiffness in her fingers. She fought with the urge to call him but she was afraid not be ignored by him again. Georgia immediately headed to Joe's restaurant to have a sincere conversation with him. Joe didn't come to work on time. Georgia sat at the table by the window so she could see him enter the restaurant. She ordered a cup of green tea and a croissant filled with raspberry jam. She kept glancing towards the window, her heart was beating like a jackhammer. Georgia was so stressed and preoccupied that she didn't feel hunger, she was too nervous to eat.

One hour has passed. Joe didn't show up. Georgia approached the waiter with a serious expression on her face. "Could you please tell me if Joe is supposed to come today?"

"I'm afraid he won't be able to come today but please, double check with him." He replied politely.

Georgia gave up waiting for him and went to the front entrance door. She stepped out of the door and accidently bumped into Joe. He instantly turned his head away, pretending to look elsewhere. Georgia grabbed his wrist. "Let me explain everything, please," she said looking directly in his eyes.

"I don't need explanations. I just asked you to be honest with me, but you lied to me. You didn't tell me that you were in a relationship with that psychopath," he said with anger in his eyes.

"My ex-boyfriend and I broke up a while ago. I unexpectedly ran into him recently. He wanted to be reunited with me. I told him that it was impossible as I was already madly in love with someone else," said Georgia with teary eyes. "I have fallen for you, Joe," she said as she tilted her head down.

Joe tipped her chin up to see her face. He pulled Georgia against him with one arm. "Senorita, you are stuck with me. You have absolutely no choice other than to be with me," he said and kissed her on her lips. "My heart bits faster when I touch your lips. You give me arrythmia," he whispered in her ear.

Joe's sweet kiss removed the burden from her shoulders. Georgia lifted her right leg in the air, she felt as if she were a little princess…

Chapter Twelve

At last, the Bollywood film shooting schedule has got finalised. Georgia's mother headed to the travel agency to book a flight ticket to India for her daughter. Entering the building, she saw her friend, Sonya standing by the window. Maria got shocked to see how different she looked. A dramatic change of hairstyle completely transformed her appearance. A very short pixy hair cut made her look younger and fresh by bringing out her features. Her hair has been dyed a garish shade of crimson. Her fashion style was also changed radically. The old-fashioned lady has turned into a modern woman. Sonya was wearing blue jeans and a heart shaped eyes emoji shirt.

"Wow! You look totally chic." Maria exclaimed in delight.

Sonya gave a snort of laughter. "It's not only my look that has altered, my life also changed totally since you saw me last." She said.

"It's great that you are open to make changes in your life that makes you happier." Said Maria.

"Well, I'm not single anymore. I have a boyfriend. He is an architect. He made me feel special and warmed my heart."

"That's terrific! You deserve a man who will make you feel loved every day."

Sonya had smiling eyes. "Life is too short to say no to chocolate and sex," she laughed with joy and booked the first available flight ticket for Georgia. "Please, don't forget to notify me of the Bollywood movie release date."

"Sure, will do." Said Maria with pride in her eyes.

Georgia's heart jumped into her throat when her mother handed her the flight ticket. She hugged it tightly to her chest. "Thanks, Mom, I can't be happier." She said with a broad smile on her face.

Georgia got in a creative mood. She lifted up the piano keyboard cover and started composing her own melody through improvisation. She wanted her piece to sound uplifting, so she chose a major scale. Her creative process was disturbed by an unexpected phone call from her old friend, Romina.

"Hi, Georgia, hope you are well." Romina sounded nervous.

Hearing her voice made Georgia utterly confused. "I'm fine, thanks. It's been a very long time since I've heard your voice," She replied.

"I'm sorry to have to tell you that our friend, Linda has passed away. She died just four days after giving birth to her baby girl." Said Romina with tears in her voice.

Georgia felt sudden weakness in her knees. The words froze in her mouth.

"Hello, can you hear me?" Romina asked her as she was silent.

"It can't be true," Georgia murmured, framing her face with her hands.

"After the birth of the baby, she had a heavy bleeding. She lost lots of blood quickly. The doctors tried to save her life; they did the best they could." Romina continued talking.

"How is the baby?" Georgia's voice shook as she asked.

"She is an adorable baby girl. She was named after her mother. I took responsibilities for her; I'm going to be her guardian."

"I can't wait to see little Linda," said Georgia and started to weep uncontrollably.

"Linda asked me to fulfil her last wish. She wanted you to be her baby's godmother." Said Romina.

Georgia cried even louder.

"Please, calm down. We have many things to organise before little Linda's christening ceremony."

"I'll do anything for her." She replied.

They agreed to meet the following day.

Georgia woke up at the crack of dawn. She poked her head out of the window to have a look at the bird's nest. Baby swallows were hardly able to fit in their nest. "Oh, my God, you have grown so big," she said to the lovely birds in a sing-song tone. In the blink of an eye, the mother swallow with her long-forked tail flew up to the nest. The bird paused for a moment, staring at the babies expectantly, as if she were telling them: 'Come on, hurry up! The little swallows flew away alongside their mother quite confidently. Georgia had a feeling they wanted to say final goodbye to her before leaving the nest. She was a little bit sad that she had missed their victorious first fly. She wanted to take a photo of the birds flying in a row, but the beautiful swallows were too fast to photograph.

A Knock on the door startled her. "Are you up yet, sweetie?" Maria stepped into her room.

"Yes, Mom."

"I know you are an early riser. I couldn't sleep, so I came to you to have a little chat," she said as she sat on the edge of the bed.

Georgia rested her head in her mother's lap. It was so quiet and peaceful, they could only hear the sound of the wall clock- tik tok, tik tok...

Georgia gasped, glancing at the clock. "Time passes so quickly with each tick of the clock. I'm saddened that I wasn't able to be with my friend, Linda when her lifetime countdown clock stopped." She said with a sigh.

"I know, dear. I'm so sorry for your loss. We get a limited time on this earth, so we need to forgive each other if we want God to forgive us for our mistakes," said Maria as she gently caressed her hair.

The clock struck nine when Georgia made her way to the baby store to get presents for Little Linda. She was looking for beautiful newborn baby clothes. There were so many nice things at the store, it was hard for her to choose the perfect gift for her future godchild. Finally, she made up her mind to purchase long sleeve cotton bodysuits, baby elephant print beanies and a cute pink dress. Then she went upstairs to the toy section. The stuffed animals were sitting together on the shelves. She grabbed the plush teddy bear off the shelf. It reminded Georgia her childhood teddy who was her secretive confidant. Whether she was in bed, eating her breakfast, or playing with her friends, the brown teddy bear was always with her. Georgia smiled, remembering her early childhood memories. Having put the plush teddy bear in the shopping basket, Georgia noticed that a curly haired little boy was staring at her with inquiring eyes. She smiled at him. The boy approached her, smiling: "The toys are bored sitting on the shelf, they feel trapped."

Georgia chuckled. "What makes you think that they are bored?" She asked.

"They are always sitting in the same position," he said with a grumpy face.

"Guess what?! I know their secret," said Georgia in a low voice. "The toys come alive at night. They dance, sing and talk to each other until early morning."

The boy's eyes widened and lit up. "Really?" He exclaimed loudly.

"Shhh!" Georgia placed her index finger vertically over her lips. "Nobody should know about it," she warned him.

"Okay, it's a top secret," said the boy, making a 'zip the lips' gesture.

Georgia kept browsing around the shop. The wooden nutcracker caught her eye. It was painted with red, green and white glitter detail. It stood on a wooden plinth and had a moving 'nutcracking' mouth. Georgia knew that a toy soldier represented power and strength and was frightening away evil spirits. She bought it for little Linda without hesitation.

When Georgia reached Romina's place, her heart started racing. She was eager to see little Linda. Romina gave her a welcoming smile.

"I've got some presents for the baby," said Georgia as she handed the large gift bag to her.

"Thank you, dear. Follow me to the nursery room and meet our angel." Said Romina.

Georgia entered the pink baby room. Little Linda was crying. Romina took the baby out of the crib and put her gently on the table to change her diaper.

"Aw, she is so tiny!" Exclaimed Georgia.

The little one stopped crying and smiled. "Her smile is so sweet. She looks like her mother." Said Georgia.

"Do you want to hold the baby?" Romina asked.

Georgia nodded, eyeing her expectantly. She held the baby at her chest level.

"Slide your hand from her bottom up to support the baby's neck." Romina advised her.

Georgia watched the baby's reactions to her touch as she was afraid not to hurt the little one. She rocked the baby in her arms and started singing a lullaby in a soft tune. Georgia was singing a song, her grandmother used to sing when she was a kid. She bonded with little Linda right away. "What is more precious in life than letting a baby nap in your arms," said Georgia in a very low voice and put her down in the crib.

Romina gave her an approving smile. They tiptoed out of the nursery room.

"Would you like to have some coffee?" Romina asked.

"Yes, please,' she replied and sat on the coach.

Georgia noticed a photo album on the table. She quickly went through it and found photos of herself from Linda's birthday party. Tears flooded her eyes. Romina entered the living room, carrying a coffee mug tray.

"We had a lot of happy memories together," said Georgia.

"Indeed, "Romina sighed with regret.

"I feel blessed that I'll be little Linda's godmother."

"I'm sure you will give her unconditional love. The christening ceremony will be held at the church on Saturday."

"It will be the new chapter of her life." Said Georgia.

They smiled lovingly at each other.

"Hey, Romina, do you still keep in touch with Morgan?" Georgia asked.

"Actually, I've not seen him for a while. I spoke to his ex-wife; she didn't know if he was dead or alive. He even didn't pay child maintenance. I'm very disappointed in him." Said Romina.

After an awkward silence, Romina glanced at her with a tight-lipped smile. A blush rushed to her cheeks. "Georgia, I was trying to find a suitable moment to talk to you. I'm deeply sorry that I turned my back on you at Morgan's insistence. He wanted to let you down and make you feel miserable. I'm ashamed that I hurt a person who has never done anything wrong to me. Please, forgive me, dear," she said, her voice was full of regret and sadness.

Georgia gave her a hug. "Let's put the past behind us. I already forgave everyone, including Morgan," she said in a quiet voice.

A few minutes later, her cell phone started ringing in her bag. Georgia grinned from ear to ear as she got a phone call from her boyfriend. She quickly left Romina's place.

"Hello, from Italy, senorita. I wish you were here with me." He said.

"I miss you so much, Joe. How are things? When are you coming back?"

"Everything is going fine; I already purchased a flight ticket to Australia. I'll see you in a couple of weeks. I promise you we will be inseparable."

"Mwah" Georgia kissed him through the phone.

"I'm dying to kiss you." said Joe as he smacked his lips over the phone and gave her a goodbye kiss.

***

Little Linda's christening ceremony was held at the small local church. Only a few close friends were invited. Linda's aunt and uncle arrived from their home country, Greece especially for the big day. Georgia was overwhelmed with joy. She pulled a gold cross necklace out of her purse and put it carefully around the baby's neck. Little Linda was wearing a white christening gown. She was smiling and shining like an angel.

"I love you so much," Georgia said to her lovely godchild.

"She loves you back." Said Romina.

The priest began the service by inviting Georgia and Romina to stand around the front. The baby was held over the basin while the priest poured water three times over her head. Little Linda stared deeply into the priest's eyes, as if she were trying to get to know him. Georgia said a prayer and lit the candle for her godchild. The baby reacted to new faces by smiling.

Georgia and Romina came out of the church. Romina was holding little Linda in her arms. She gazed into the baby's sparkling eyes, showing a sweet motherly tenderness towards her. The beautiful rainbow arched across the sky. It seemed to have been raining. The sky was filled with splendid colours: Purple, green, blue, yellow and orange.

"Wow! What a magnificent rainbow." Exclaimed Georgia.

"Yes, indeed," said Romina with a thoughtful expression on her face.

"See, the sun appeared after the rain. Our friend left us forever, though her daughter has brightened our lives, she gave us hope," said Georgia and looked at the baby fondly.

"You are right, dear. Little Linda gave us a reason to smile and made our lives better." Replied Romina.

After the religious ceremony, the guests headed to Romina's place to hold a celebration. The living room was beautified with colourful balloons. Linda's relatives sat around the dining table, which was decorated with flower vases and scented candles. Linda's aunt was a middle-aged woman with a plump face and wide neck. She was wearing a pearl necklace, sitting up high on her throat. It seemed that a tight fitted necklace around her neck was preventing her to breathe normally. Her husband was a tall man with broad shoulders. He was wearing a black kangol hat and oval shaped eyeglasses.

"Little Linda resembles her mother," said Linda's aunt as she held the tiny baby for the first time. "Linda was like a daughter to me. I'd like to look after the child, she is my flash and blood. I want her to live with me in Greece." She gently rubbed the baby's soft head.

Romina got frustrated. Her facial muscles became tense. "I totally understand your concern, but Linda appointed me in her will as the child's guardian. She trusted me with her baby." Said Romina with desperation in her voice.

"I know that you work full time for a middle-class salary, dear. You don't have enough money to pamper the child. I'm available round the clock to look after little Linda. Besides, I can afford to hire a nanny for the baby." said Linda's aunt and rubbed her pearls between her hands to loosen them up.

Little Linda started crying loudly. She sensed the nervous tension in the room. Georgia glanced at her with a worried look on her face. "The baby must be tired, if you don't mind, I'll put her to bed." She said.

"Sure," replied Linda's aunt and kissed the baby on her tiny foot.

Georgia took little Linda to the nursery room. She swayed the baby rhythmically from side to side and sang the dearest lullaby to her.

Romina and Linda's aunt couldn't agree with each other on the delicate matter. Romina kept arguing with her. "I think you don't love this baby; you just want to use her as a trophy kid. You see her as an extension of yourself." Said Romina with tears in her eyes.

"How dare you talk to me like that?!" Linda's aunt shouted. Her husband looked embarrassed. He elbowed her mildly in attempt to stop her being rude.

Georgia rushed into the living room to neutralize the tension. "We can't decide this sensitive matter just based on wealth. We need to make a decision in the best interests of the child. Romina is like a mother to little Linda. She has established a strong bond with her. The baby has already lost her mother, please, don't let her loose her second mom," said Georgia with a pleading tone.

Her words made powerful effect on everyone. Linda's uncle apologised to Romina for hurting her feelings.

"I'm really sorry for a misunderstanding, Romina. I see you truly love the baby. I will support my grandchild financially till the end of my life. I just need to ask you a favour: Please, let the child learn her mother tongue, let her visit our home country and respect our culture and traditions," said Linda's uncle as he shook hands with Romina.

"I promise you that little Linda will make you proud." replied Romina.

Linda's aunt started crying. Romina sat on the coach next to her. "I'm sorry for overreacting. You are welcome to visit us anytime you want." She said.

"Thank you. I appreciate your understanding." She replied.

Georgia put the christening cake on the table. The cake was decorated with a pink rose swirl cross. Linda's uncle placed a slice of delicious cake on his plate. "Well, I've started a special weight loss program. My wife doesn't allow me to eat sweets, but today I'm going to be very naughty," he said and licked the cream covered fork.

Everyone laughed heartily…

Chapter Thirteen

Georgia woke up hearing her parents talking loudly. She felt too lazy to get out of bed. She threw the pillow over her head, but she couldn't block out the noise. Georgia heard the footsteps approaching her door. A few seconds later, her father poked his head into her room: "Sweetie, are you awake?" He asked.

"Yeah, come on in, Dad." Replied Georgia.

Daniel was holding a newspaper in his hands. He sat in the arm chair beside her bed. "I don't want you to panic, but a life-threatening virus is spreading across the globe. You should be careful, please, don't leave home without wearing a face mask," he said in a worried voice and handed her a newspaper.

Georgia became anxious as she read the article about the deadly virus. She got shocked to find out that the millions of people were sent into lockdown over virus surge. "Oh, my God! I can't believe my eyes," said Georgia, folding the newspaper.

"We need to face the difficulties in life, dear." Said Daniel. "People have been asked not to leave their homes except for essential needs. Our favourite restaurants shuttered their doors and unfortunately all international flights have been suspended," he said with a sigh and walked out of the room.

Georgia felt depressed. She looked like a popped balloon. 'I had so many goals to achieve in life,' she murmured to herself. 'Not so fast, Georgia,' responded the universe...

Opening the top drawer of her desk, she took out the flight ticket and stared at it with sadness in her eyes.

There were three days left until she was supposed to leave for India, but it seemed life had other plans. She realised that her future was uncertain. Tears rolling down her cheeks, soaked the dream ticket. Georgia felt lonely. She desperately needed to hear her boyfriend's voice, who was in Italy spending time with his family. Georgia called Joe to make sure that he was doing fine. Joe sounded like he wasn't well, he was coughing and breathing heavily. It seemed the air was stuck in his lungs. He said that he had been self-isolating at home, waiting for the virus test result. Georgia got stressed out but she hid her anxiety as she didn't want to leave him worried. She encouraged him to be more optimistic and wished him a speedy recovery.

A terrible fear sneaked up right behind Georgia and locked her in chokehold. She knew that only the astrologer could help her to get rid of negative emotions, so she decided to give him a visit. On the way to the Astrologer's house, Georgia dropped by the pharmacy to buy a face mask. New policies limited the amount of people inside the store. The customers stood in a queue outside, keeping physical distance from each other. After waiting patiently in a queue for nearly half an hour, she finally entered the store.

"Can I have a face mask, please?" She asked the pharmacist.

"You are lucky, there is only one left," he said and gave her a light blue face mask.

Their conversation was interrupted by an old woman leaning on a cane. She furrowed her brows with concern. "Jesus Christ! Don't you have any in stock?" She asked the pharmacist with fear in her eyes.

"No, unfortunately not, ma'am." He replied.

The old woman's face paled even more. Her wrinkled hands started shaking. Georgia felt uncomfortable. "Please, don't worry about it. You can have mine," she said and gave the old woman her newly purchased face mask.

The old woman looked at her with grateful eyes. "Oh, dear, thank you," she said. She quickly put on her face mask and sighed in relief. It made her feel safe and secure.

Georgia pulled the scarf from her neck and covered her face. She reached the astrologer's place downhearted and discouraged. The astrologer greeted her as he opened the front door. "The scarf won't protect you against infections disease, dear." He said.

"I know, I couldn't manage to buy a face mask. I will definitely get it later." She replied.

The astrologer walked her into the living room. He opened the top drawer of his desk and took out a fresh cotton mask. "It's for you, dear. It comes with three layers of protective material and fits easily around the ears," said the astrologer and handed it to her.

"Thank you so much. It's so kind of you." Said Georgia.

The astrologer offered her a cup of green tea. "You need to keep your body warm inside. The hot tea will soothe stress and anxiety." He said.

Georgia drank her tea in one gulp and carefully put the glass back on the table. She sighed a deep, despairing sigh. "I'm worried that the world may end in a viral disease." She said.

The astrologer frowned at her. "I'm surprised to hear that from you. I thought you were much braver."

"It seems I'm not brave enough, I'm not that thick skinned. My life has turned upside down. I think my boyfriend might be infected as he is already showing symptoms of virus." Said Georgia.

"Believe in power of prayer, accept the reality and shield yourself with faith." Said the astrologer.

"I'm trying to think positive, but I'm still struggling to cope with fear."

"I know why it happens. You are looking in the wrong direction. Do you understand what I'm saying?"

"I understand, but my mind and my heart are in conflict."

"You need to follow your deep heart; it will guide you where you need to go. At this point your debater mind will take a backseat. The evil spirit can easily crawl into the human brain, but it can never enter your heart,' he said. His gaze was calm and intense.

She listened to his words attentively, though she couldn't' absorb them fully. She told him her whole story, touching her old wounds.

"Georgia, you shouldn't be threatened or afraid of challenges in life. God will never give you more than you can handle. You need to start developing self-realisation and get enjoyment out of the present moment. To be honest, I'm little bit disappointed in you. You said that somebody tried to kill you and you were devastated. But you are still alive, isn't that reason enough to be happy? You didn't even mention that you were grateful to God," he said with a thoughtful expression on his face.

Georgia was quiet for a few moments, collecting her thoughts. She looked at the astrologer with a fixed stare, her lips were partially open. She was embarrassed and ashamed of herself for not seeing the good in the bad. In a split second, her whole life flashed before her eyes. She realised that she has never been alone, her guardian angel has been always protecting her. "Maybe I'm stuck in the past," she said with a sigh. "Sometimes I 'm genuinely afraid of the future and I don't give myself permission to live in the moment and enjoy it," she let her soul speak.

"I'm happy that you took a dive into the depths of your soul. I recommend you to do a daily meditation. Don't try to influence your thoughts, trust your inner gut, just go with the flow. Your mind will be free from all distractions; you will get the power of intuition. You will not absorb other people's energy. You will control your mind." Said the astrologer, his voice was persuasive.

"You are so true. I need to look in the right direction and get hope back in my life. Can I meditate now?" She asked.

The astrologer smiled warmly. "Of course, you can," he replied.

She sat down on the carpeted floor cross legged and started meditating. Georgia closed her eyes, breathing slowly in and out. She listened to her inner voice, it brought positive energy to her. She crushed her fear like a crystal vase and finally felt at peace. "I'm tired of always trying to avoid life's bumps, looking for an escape.

Now I'm ready to face challenges in life. My heart knows the way. It will tell me everything I need to know." She said to the astrologer.

"I'm glad that you opened your heart to hope," Said the astrologer and smiled with his eyes.

"I really appreciate your willingness to support me whenever I need. I'm so grateful to you," said Georgia and left his place.

The weather was beautiful. The sun's rays penetrated deeply into her skin and warmed her bones. Georgia decided to enjoy a stroll through the park. It was quiet, she could easily hear the chirping sounds of the birds. Georgia gingerly sat down on a narrow bench. She was a little carried away by her thoughts when a tiny flying beetle landed on her hand without her permission. It was red with black dots.

"Oh, dear ladybug, where did you come from, huh?!" She exclaimed. "If you leave my hand and fly off, my love will return back to me." Georgia made a wish. In a blink of an eye, the lady bug flew away. Georgia's face shone with joy. She headed home; her heart filled with thankfulness.

Entering her apartment building, she bumped into her Indian neighbour, Rasheed. He was wearing a black face mask, matching to his blue turban. Georgia got excited to see him. "Hello, Rasheed Ji. How are you doing?"

He wobbled his head softly. "I'm fine, thanks for asking. I hope this pandemic will be over soon."

"Well, I choose not to lose hope. How is your wife?"

"She is good, self-isolating at home."

Georgia was about to enter the elevator when she noticed a sign posted on the wall saying: 'Please, maintain 1.5 metres psychical distance from each other.' In the tiny elevator there wouldn't be enough space to keep distance, so she let her neighbour take a ride first. Georgia pressed the call button again. Stepping into the elevator, she fixed her face mask in the mirror. The door was almost shut when a tall, pensionable- aged man forced it to remain open. He rushed into the elevator, joining her. Georgia was concerned as he ignored the social distancing rules. A few seconds later, the elevator got stuck at a point between the third and fourth floors. The man panicked when he realised that he was trapped in a metal box. His eyes almost popped out of their sockets with fear. His heart was pounding at an increasingly rapid pace. He ripped off his mask and screamed for help. He shouted as loud as he could. The bubbly saliva flowed out of his mouth unintentionally.

"Please, calm down," said Georgia. She pressed the alarm button and waited for the call centre worker to pick up.

The man was uncontrollably irrational from fear. He unbuttoned his shirt as he had shortness of breath. "I have a phobia of being trapped in a small space. I never take an elevator alone. If someone leaves before me, I walk out of the elevator and climb stairs to reach my apartment on the eleventh floor."

"I understand, everything will be alright. You are not alone." She said in a calm tone.

When she got through to the call centre, the operator instructed her that the engineer would be on the way as soon as possible.

"See, it will be over soon. All we have to do is wait. The problem won't be solved by screaming loudly. No matter how much we protest, the engineer isn't going to be here any faster. We just need to focus on something else other than the fear. Actually, taking a few mediative breaths can ground the mind." Said Georgia.

"I'm thankful to God that I'm not alone, otherwise I would have gone crazy." He said in an agitated tone.

"Just close your lips and breathe in through your nose slowly until your lungs are full. Focus on positive things and let go of fear." She said.

The man slightly closed his eyes, willing himself to be calm. They started breathing together, he was imitating her movements. Deep breathing helped his nervous system. " I feel so much better. I think I got rid of numbness in my palm and fingers." He said.

"I'm glad to hear that you are feeling better." She replied.

When the engineer arrived, the man was already calmed down. "So good that I managed to control my bladder for the entire duration." He chuckled softly. "Meditation saved my life. I think today I overcame my phobia of being alone in the elevator. Thank you so much for being a good neighbour." He said to her as he buttoned up his shirt.

With life at a standstill, panic around the disease has been increased and the deep depression around the world has started. Georgia did her best to stay calm and rational. She followed all precautionary safety measures recommended by health professionals. She freed herself of the fear of future and began accepting the reality. She found comfort through adaptive thoughts. Georgia started appreciating things more such as: handshake with a stranger, full shelves in the store, crowded theatres, coffee with a friend...

On her regular trip to the supermarket, Georgia couldn't find a single roll of toilet paper. It was something she had never seen before. A fear of the deadly virus has sent the country into a toilet paper buying hysteria. Georgia brought some fruit and vegetables from the market. A shop assistant put her stuff into a plastic bag. "Thank you very much, hope you are doing well." Said Georgia to her.

"Oh, I'm not well. I can't cope with the stress." She replied in a trembling voice.

Georgia noticed that the shop assistant's eye whites were enlarged. She was pale with dark circles under her eyes. "The suffering will fade away," She tried to calm her down. Georgia abruptly turned around as she heard the sound of hands clapping. She saw two paramedics in blue uniforms standing in the middle of the crowd.

"Thank you for risking your lives to save ours," said the shop assistant to them.

The paramedics smiled and waved at her.

"You are real heroes! "Exclaimed the old woman from the crowd.

The paramedics looked calm and in control. "It's our duty to be on the front line of the pandemic," said one of the them.

Georgia was touched. She had a melancholy smile on her face. Grabbing her bag, she took a step forward. All of a sudden, she got struck by a paper airplane. She turned her head and saw Morgan's twin daughters standing there, with their hands in their pockets. They were wearing colourful face masks. "Hey, Georgia, let's make a bet! Can you tell which one of us is Sylvia?" Asked the girl wearing a pink cotton mask.

Georgia smiled at them. There was an expression of carefree happiness in their eyes. Their appearance brightened up her gloomy day. "What are we betting on?" She asked.

"We are betting on chocolate."

"All right, but why are you here alone?"

"Our mom is standing in a long queue to pay for the groceries."

Georgia came closer to them. Having put the bag at her feet, she inspected them closely, but she couldn't find the clue, the mole on the cheek as their faces were covered with masks. She responded without conscious thought: "The girl wearing a pink mask is Sylvia."

"You lost the bet!" Exclaimed Sophia in delight. She took off her pink mask, there was no mole on her cheek. The girl chuckled loudly, showing her missing upper tooth.

"Girls, you really deserve a prize," said Georgia and ran to the candy section.

After a few minutes, she returned holding the chocolate bars. The twins were standing next to a blonde woman.

"You must be Georgia. Kids have told me a lot about you. I'm their mom." She said, smiling. Her eyes looked tired.

"Nice to meet you, your kids are adorable," she replied, handing them the chocolate bars.

"Thank you!" The girls exclaimed with one voice.

"You are welcome." Replied Georgia.

The twin's mother pushed the shopping trolly towards the exit. The kids hopped on one leg, tousling each other's hair. It was a fun sight for Georgia, she smiled behind her mask.

She took the grocery bags home and straight away went to the small church, where little Linda has been christened. The church was temporally closed to slow the virus outbreak. It made her sad. She sat down on the top of the stairs in front of the beautiful, old church. She took a moment to pray in her heart. She prayed for her boyfriend's well-being. When she said the final words of the prayer, she got a phone call from Joe. "Hello, senorita. I'm crying with happiness. I've just received a negative test result; I'm virus free."

"Thank God. This is the best news I've heard lately." She replied, happy tears ran down her cheeks.

Georgia read a prayer of gratitude at home and lit candles to hon-our people who have died and those who were helping the sick during the pandemic. Daily meditation practise helped her to become more self-aware, it increased her patience and tolerance. She returned to her old self. She became happy and bubbly. Georgia stayed several months at home. She was physically active during self- isolation, she kept herself entertained. She followed an online exercise class, read lots of interesting books, watched new TV series, and even made a balcony garden. She created her little fragrant oasis. Georgia started growing sunflowers, happy flowers on her balcony to bring joy to her life. She was pampering them, singing and talking to her plants to help them grow faster. Georgia didn't allow her dog to enter the garden as Oscar loved digging up the plants.

Within a few short weeks, the plants started growing. The sun sent its rays to them. The adorable flowers made Georgia's balcony look nice and cosy. It gave her an amazing feeling to take care of the plants. Georgia was excited to see the result of the hard work. "Mom, my flowers are blooming!" She exclaimed.

"Oh, dear, good on you. They are adorable." Replied Maria.

While Georgia was busy with taking photos of her houseplants, Oscar took a chance and rushed into the balcony as the door has been left ajar. The happy dog began running back and forth with his tongue out.

Georgia noticed her dog urinating on the plants. "Oscar, shame on you!" She said in a firm voice. Oscar got embarrassed. He pinned his ears down, furrowed his brows and looked up at her with guilty eyes. The dog genuinely apologised for doing a bad thing by nudging Georgia's hand. It was his way of saying sorry. Georgia couldn't resist the urge to smile. Since the incident, Oscar has never tried to enter the balcony garden.

Little by little, pandemic restrictions have slightly eased as the situation has improved. The scientists began working on a vaccine against the new virus. It gave people a hope for the future. The lockdown has been lifted. Georgia was happy that life started slowly returning to normal. After two months sitting at home, she finally took off her pyjamas. She even forgot how did it feel like wearing a dress. Georgia opened her wardrobe and looked at her dresses hanging sadly on hangers. Her clothes looked faded. Georgia grabbed the hanger with a red dress. She sniffed the dress, the scent of perfume still lingered on it. It was the same dress she wore on a first date with Joe. She put on her red dress and did a twirl in front of the square shaped mirror.

Georgia went to the coffee shop on reopening day. Her favourite place looked a little bit different with fewer tables. Even with restrictions, being able to drink coffee at the coffee shop was a joy for her. She noticed an old couple sitting at the table in front of each other, drinking coffee.

They were holding hands tightly. Georgia closed her eyes and imagined herself as an old woman sitting at the café, drinking coffee with her boyfriend, Joe. In her imagination they both had grey hair and wrinkled hands. Their hearts were full of love.

The sound of the phone ringing snapped her out of her daydream. Georgia was glad to hear her drama school friend, Jessica's voice. "Hi, G. I hope you are fine. I'm organising a birthday party at my place next Saturday. I'd love to invite you."

"Oh, thanks a lot, Jess. I missed you so much. I'm looking forward to attending your party."

"You are welcome. There is one condition, though."

"And what is your condition?"

"Everyone who is going to attend the party has to bring a negative virus test result."

Her response made Georgia almost choke on a sip of coffee. She started coughing.

"Hey, wait a sec! Why are you coughing, are you sure you are okay?" Jessica's voice sounded concerned.

"I'm alright." She replied.

"Georgia, I think you better stay at home. You can attend my birthday party next year. Please, stay safe and healthy," she said and ended the conversation.

Georgia looked puzzled. When she realised what just happened, she began laughing softy to herself.

Georgia headed to the church to attend the Sunday mess. She was glad to see the church door open. She knelt down and prayed with all her heart. She thanked God for giving her strength during the most difficult time. Her tranquillity was disturbed by a phone ringtone. Georgia thought that Jessica has changed her mind and was going to invite her to the party without any conditions. Pulling her phone out of the bag, she saw the film director's name on the screen display. She rushed out of the church to answer his call.

"Hello, Georgia. Hope you are doing well." He said.

"Hello, Avinaj Ji. I'm delighted to hear your voice. How is everything going?"

"By God's grace we will continue film shooting soon. Wait a little while and we will meet again. We are not going to make just a movie; we are going to make a history." He encouraged her.

Georgia had been anticipating this moment for a while. After a heart touching conversation with the film director, she got so emotional that she burst into tears. The moment she entered the church, she felt safe. She felt the majesty of Jesus Christ, his greatness, his love for her. Something stirred inside her, it was a soul shaking experience. She got lost in sweet acapella songs…

The End